POLYGRAM FILMED ENTERTAINMENT PRESENTS

A PROPAGANDA FILMS PRODUCTION

A DAVID FINCHER FILM

MICHAEL DOUGLAS SEAN PENN

"THE GAME"

JAMES REBHORN PETER DONAT CARROLL BAKER

AND ARMIN MUELLER-STAHL CASTING BY DON PHILLIPS

CO-PRODUCERS JOHN BRANCATO AND MICHAEL FERRIS

EXECUTIVE PRODUCERS ANDREW KEVIN WALKER JONATHAN MOSTOW

COSTUME DESIGNER MICHAEL KAPLAN MUSIC BY HOWARD SHORE

EDITOR JAMES HAYGOOD PRODUCTION DESIGN BY JEFFREY BEECROFT

DIRECTOR OF PHOTOGRAPHY HARRIS SAVIDES

PRODUCED BY STEVE GOLIN AND CEÁN CHAFFIN

WRITTEN BY JOHN BRANCATO & MICHAEL FERRIS

DIRECTED BY DAVID FINCHER

PolyGram

FILMED ENTERTAINMENT
DISTRIBUTION

the GAME

A David Fincher Film

A novel by
JEFF ROVIN

Based on the film written by
John Brancato & Michael Ferris

BOULEVARD BOOKS, NEW YORK

THE GAME

A Boulevard Book / published by arrangement with
Polygram Filmed Entertainment, Inc.

PRINTING HISTORY
Boulevard edition / September 1997

The Putnam Berkley World Wide Web site address is
http://www.berkley.com

ISBN: 1-57297-328-5

BOULEVARD
Boulevard Books are published by The Berkley Publishing Group,
a member of Penguin Putnam Inc.,
200 Madison Avenue, New York, New York 10016.
BOULEVARD and its logo are trademarks
belonging to Berkley Publishing Corporation.

PRINTED IN THE UNITED STATES OF AMERICA

10 9 8 7 6 5 4 3 2 1

the
GAME

There are no sounds as magical as those of an 8mm projector.

The driving hum of the motor, the chatter of the teeth as they draw the film from the reel, the heart-stopping tug-snap when a splice runs through the gate. The unnatural silence of the images. An 8mm projector is an old-fashioned engine that transports you into the past: a warm and inviting past where everyone was on their best behavior and only the moment mattered—the birthday party, the graduation, Christmas morning.

The quiet, pale-color images played out on the silvery-white screen. Nicholas Van Orton had resisted transferring the two-hundred-foot reels to video because this way the images were slightly larger than life. Just like romanticized memories were supposed to be. He also hadn't seen the pictures in years—so many years that it was like seeing them fresh.

He saw the two-story brick mansion where he and his younger brother Conrad grew up. The balcony from which they threw paper airplanes until the perfect green lawn was littered with them. The hedges in whose soil they set up plastic soldiers—"men" they called them in those blissfully, politically unaware times—and pretended they were in the Ardennes fighting the Battle of the Bulge. The trees they used to climb and hang from and play Revolutionary War sniper in (especially after Nicholas read *Johnny Tremain* in school).

Nicholas watched, chin in hand, as the wonderful old Scottish butler McIver crossed the expansive lawn. Nicholas loved McIver, who told wonderful bedtime stories about his years with the Highland Division facing Rommel's vaunted Afrika Korps. McIver was with them until Conrad left home. His first name was Robin, and Nicholas remembered once when his father had to go out one Sunday and "fix" something because McIver had broken the nose of a man who had called him a sissy. McIver didn't get along very well with their Austrian nanny, Ilsa. He used to call her "Hon" under his breath. It wasn't until years later that Nicholas realized he was calling her "Hun."

In McIver's big hands was a huge, square birthday cake with lighted sparklers. As he approached the camera, distinguished-looking young men in suits and crew cuts and women in cat's-eye sunglasses stepped back. The crowd of twenty-odd people were singing "Happy Birthday" and clapping out the cadence—singing and clapping silently, like ghosts.

Some of them probably are ghosts, Nicholas thought. He was watching his seventh birthday party, nearly forty-one years ago. That would put many of his parents' guests in their late sixties to early seventies today. A few of them were almost certainly gone. Yet there they were, happily unacquainted with the car crash or cancer or addiction that was going to end their life.

You never know what's going to get you, do you? he thought as he looked at them all so young and hale and confident.

Nicholas watched as children followed the cake. They

2

were all wearing party hats. The boys were in dark suits, which made them look older, and the girls were in fluffy pastel dresses with bows, which made them look like princesses. They moved like the segments of a centipede, weaving in and out of the camera's view, behind McIver. Nicholas recognized the scrubbed and smiling face of Albert Bundonis, who had been his best friend. They lost touch when Albert joined the Marines. But there he was in the front of the line, marching like a little soldier even then. He was followed by Janet Douglas, and Timothy Michaels, who didn't seem at all happy with his hat and kept running his finger under the tight elastic band. Next came Tommy Fitzpatrick, who stuck his thumbs in his ears, poked out his tongue, and made a face at the camera. Ron Plummer and Alice Newcomb brought up the rear. Nicholas had had a major crush on Alice. She was the only girl he knew who liked comic books.

They were all so important to his life, then. Where were they today? Were all of *them* still alive?

The children stopped and gathered in a circle around Nicholas, who was wearing a blindfold.

Cut to his mother, youthful and lovely and smiling. Nicholas calculated quickly. She was twenty-eight then. Her world was the house and her three men. She seemed content. He suspected that she was.

His mother pointed to Nicholas and the camera followed. She removed the blindfold. Nicholas ogled the cake. It was funny. He remembered his Grandmother Rose taking him to the movies as a present. She took him to see a movie called *It Came from Beneath the Sea*. It was about a giant octopus that destroyed San Francisco. The size and power of the creature had made a big impression on him. And seeing familiar landmarks in his hometown destroyed excited him. He didn't know why, but it did.

Yet as he watched this movie, he couldn't remember

seeing the cake through his eyes. Only through the camera lens. It was as if the real event had never happened.

Nicholas watched as his mother fussed over his hair, fixing it where the blindfold had mussed it. He reached for a sparkler.

Cut to his father. The camera wasn't steady anymore; his mother was taking the pictures. There was a dizzying pan to McIver cutting the cake, then another rocket-fast pan back to Father. He was sitting on a folding chair, smoking a cigarette as he observed the proceedings. He was wearing a frown on his thin, deeply lined face. His bright blue party hat served to emphasize the dark intensity of his expression. Father looked older than his thirty-four years.

Hell, Nicholas thought. *He looks older than I do now.*

Maybe that was because he was Father. For some reason Nicholas had never quite adjusted to the idea that he himself was a man. But his father was one. He wielded strong, silent authority. Even McIver seemed afraid of him.

The elder Van Orton jabbed out his cigarette in the crystal ashtray that rested on his thigh. Then he put it on the ground and rose. He'd never once looked at the camera.

His father was back behind the lens. The picture was steady again as a Harlequin clown made balloon animals. His smile and gestures were large and happy. Young Nicholas was not. He handed the completed animals out, obviously annoyed that his friends were not paying attention to him but were now comfortable with the camera. The girls were all posing and the boys were turning and mugging for posterity. Tommy's thumbs were still in his ears and his tongue was still darting in and out. Nicholas watched himself mouth Tommy's name in frustration. Tommy turned around long enough to accept his balloon animal and put it on top of his party hat. Then he faced the camera again with his thumbs back in his ears.

Watching the movie, Nicholas experienced a flash of the

frustration his young self must have felt. There was always someone who just couldn't get with the program.

Mother was back behind the camera. The picture moved jerkily to her friends, blowing cigarette smoke and vamping. Their lipstick was so red, so perfect. So were their nails. They were watching the kids eat cake. The girls got the icing roses, of course. The camera swept to his father holding a piece of birthday cake. A plastic fork was stuck in the top and the cake was untouched. A man Nicholas didn't recognize was talking to Father, who was staring down, unblinking. Nicholas remembered that distracted look very well. He wondered if his father was ever happy. Had Nicholas's mother ever pleased him, really? Had he? Had Conrad?

One of his mother's friends—Mrs. Haveles, her name popped into his head—held a plate of cake with a rose toward the lens. The world turned around as the camera was put down, still running as his mother forgot to remove her finger from the button.

The picture resumed again some time later. The picture was low; Nicholas had been permitted to take the camera.

Not bad, he thought proudly as he watched the scenery pass slowly, steadily. The sunlight was different and the servants were clearing the tables under McIver's watchful gaze. Lame balloon animals littered the chairs, trees, and lawn. Nicholas's flagging but undaunted mother was still smiling. Now she was trying to get his father to smile for the camera. She got behind him, shook her long hair out of the way, and rested her chin on his left shoulder. She put her arms around his chest. He leaned forward and smiled flatly, dutifully.

Another day. Ilsa, looking very young in her white nanny uniform, was holding an infant toward the camera. Conrad looked about a month old. He was crying and drooling. Nodding to an off-camera instruction—she did what she was told when she was told to do it, even then—Ilsa turned to her left. Nicholas was sitting on the sofa and, bending, she gently placed the baby in his waiting arms. He cradled the boy carefully. After a moment Conrad stopped crying. Nicholas looked up at the camera and smiled contentedly.

Conrad content, Nicholas thought. *And because of something I did.* That *was* one for the time capsule.

Another year. Nicholas was older now, about nine or ten. Conrad was two or three. The boys were playing tag on the lawn, Conrad laughing with his entire face as his brother chased him down. God, Nicholas could almost hear his high, delighted squeals. That was Connie: always one for fun. The camera was following them like a springer spaniel; Mom was shooting. She suddenly landed on Dad and stopped. He was walking toward the house. He turned abruptly as though he'd been called. Then he walked backward, away from the camera, giving a small wave until he reached the front door.

Another time. Conrad's birthday. His third, according to the big wax "3" candle on the cake. Nicholas had a Rootie Kazootie puppet on his right hand and his nemesis, Poison Zoomack, on his left. He was performing for Conrad and his friends. The oversized rubber Rootie head had a baseball cap turned to the right and a big, goofy smile between a smattering of freckles. Nicholas could vividly remember the vinyl smell of that head. He could still feel the stiff gray fabric of Rootie's arms on his fingers. He didn't remember Zoomack very well, but then Zoomack was the bad guy. He always got punched right off the left hand and tended to stay on the ground, where he hit.

It was easy to tell bad guys then, wasn't it? Nicholas asked himself.

The mouth of the screen—Nicholas was moving silently. The kids were laughing. Suddenly, Rootie punched Zoomack and he went flying. Rootie and Nicholas both faced the camera and took a bow. Nicholas wasn't smiling. He had a job to do and he was serious about it, even then.

The screen went white. The end of the film flap-flap-flapped against the projector. Nicholas leaned back toward the den coffee table. He threw the switch on the base and the machine stopped.

The smell of the warm projector engine filled the still air long after the show had ended. So did the memories, which were warm and comforting. So did the visions of a world that was so safe and full of promise. A world in which Davy Crockett and *The Adventures of Superman* ruled TV and the Hardy Boys ruled his bookshelf. A world of flipping baseball cards with his friends. (He smiled. He knew just the right technique to get face or back. Cleaned out the other kids, every time. Still did, only now when they played with Topps or Fleer, it was the companies, not the cards, they made.)

Forty-one years ago tomorrow. When the postwar world was young and so was Nicholas.

When he smiled because he was glad, not because he'd beaten some dumb bastard in a corporate war.

When he still believed that you could count on someone other than your own damn self.

chapter 2

What a difference forty-one years makes, Nicholas thought as he studied his face in the mirror. The bulbs in rows on either side of the mirror were severe critics, throwing shadows in every wrinkle. But still. He didn't see much of the child left in the man.

The once full, red cheeks were drawn now. Not exactly hollow, but not as full of vigor as they should be. The dark eyes were very dark and the longish black hair, while it was all still there, was thinning in the front and graying over the ears and across the sides. The chin sagged a little, and not with the remnants of baby fat. The thin-lipped mouth, once merry and glad to be the voice of a puppet, was now chronically downturned, it seemed. Now he commanded puppets, which wasn't nearly the same thing.

His chest was tight—the lights brought out the barest hint of shreds along his shoulders—and his upper arms were strong because he worked out every morning. Free weights on the bedroom floor, not the kid stuff with pulleys and cables and a soft, padded bench to lie on.

Two years from today you'll be fifty, he thought as he

turned his electric shaver on and guided it around his face. He took a little extra time with the deep cleft in his chin.

Fifty. A half century. That was a long damn time. Yet inside a big part of him still felt like the kid he'd watched in the movie. Wanting to run around on the lawn, climb a tree, watch someone do something he couldn't, like make balloon animals. Hell, he remembered the flash of excitement he always got when he was able to stretch a balloon and get that first breath to stay in there instead of blowing spit on a limp rubber sac. In its own way, blowing up a balloon was almost as gratifying as a successful IPO.

He replaced the shaver in the holder, splashed on some aftershave, then walked back into the bedroom. He opened the top dresser drawer and, while he put on his heavily starched white shirt, he looked at the framed photographs sitting on top of the dresser. His mother and father, from when they were newlyweds to when they'd been long married. Himself when he was a baby, an entrepreneur with a fresh-squeezed orange juice stand (all the other kids competed for the limited lemonade trade), a college graduate. There were also photographs of him and Conrad and two wedding pictures of his former wife Elizabeth.

Nicholas lingered on the wallet-sized pictures in their hinged frame. He wondered if Elizabeth would call today. She had never forgotten his birthday, but he hadn't taken her call the last two years. It was too painful, too bittersweet talking to her. To go into a relationship with so much love and so much hope and to have it come apart—

Marriage is like an overstuffed sandwich, his brother had once put it. *You love all the ingredients but the damn thing just doesn't hold together.* Conrad could be amusing when he wanted to be. Now that he thought of it, Conrad had always liked Elizabeth. And she'd liked him. Maybe the two of them should have gotten together.

But that would have required Conrad to stay put. At a rehab center, if nothing else.

Nicholas did his silk tie in a small, tight knot then walked over to the night table. He slipped a heavy, gold Patek Phillipe watch on his right wrist—crystal on the bottom of his wrist to protect it. He checked the time.

It was 6:32. Two minutes too much nostalgia. He walked briskly from the room and down the carpeted stairs.

Breakfast was waiting where he liked it: in the corner of the large kitchen island. Three eggs, sunny-side up, Canadian bacon and two slices of rye toast lightly buttered, a large glass of fresh-squeezed orange juice, cool and tangy. He'd have coffee at the office. He tossed his tie over his shoulder to protect it and read the newspaper as he stood eating. Outside the sliding glass door, old Ilsa moved slowly through the garden, cutting flowers. She had acknowledged Nicholas's arrival with a curt little bow. Nicholas had waved back.

After eating everything except the toast and glancing at the headlines—except for the business section, which he read carefully—he slipped on his sunglasses, slung his laptop case over his shoulder, and headed to the sliding glass door. He stepped into a spectacular spring morning with just the hint of lingering night chill. The sun drove that away as he walked toward the garden.

"The toast looked a little well done, Ilsa," he said as he strode past. "You get that taste in your mouth, it's there for the day."

"I'm very sorry, sir," she replied. "The toaster oven hasn't been itself."

"Get a new one."

"I will. Have a pleasant day. And happy birthday, Mr. Van Orton."

"Thank you." He looked back without stopping and scowled. "No one's planning any surprise parties, are they, Ilsa?"

"Not that I'm aware of, sir," she said.

Nicholas nodded. Chances were that if any of his friends

were planning anything, they wouldn't have told Ilsa. Because then she would have told him. Her first loyalty was to her employer.

"Fine," he said. "See you later."

Nicholas walked quickly down the curving stone pathway to where his BMW 750 sat in the circular driveway. He checked his watch again. If he hurried, he could still beat the traffic. He climbed in, fired the engine up, then headed toward the large gateway.

God, he hoped no one was planning a party. If there were one thing he hated it was surprise anythings. He hated being unprepared.

The ghosts of balloon animals were everywhere across the lawn. He popped them, mentally. He didn't have time for more memories. He had a financial empire to run. Popping in his CD of Horowitz playing the Chopin Etudes, he drove along the winding roads from his Pacific Heights estate. As the San Francisco skyline appeared above the morning fog, he gazed out at the sparkling waters of the Bay. He thought of the giant octopus from the film. He remembered feeling excited when the military killed the creature with some kind of special torpedo fired in its brain. He felt good not because the menace was destroyed but because the men who did it had power. They had more power than the giant octopus and that was pretty impressive to a seven-year-old.

Nicholas changed lanes freely and rarely slipped below sixty-five miles an hour. Tickets didn't bother him: they were the price of doing business. And the business was living as fast as he liked. There were no citations today as he zipped through the early morning traffic. He headed through Nob Hill and continued east into the Financial District, to his building on Montgomery Street. It was located almost exactly on the spot where Sam Brannan had discovered gold in 1848 and started the California Gold Rush. Nicholas loved that fact not because he was a history buff—he wasn't—but because he was a science buff. And he'd proved that lightning could strike the same place twice.

The firm's corporate headquarters was located in a sturdy old brownstone bookended by towering glass skyscrapers. During the 1989 earthquake, those babies had rained windows all over the place. His building, home of the Van Orton Group—and some of the smartest brokers money could buy *and* hold—only lost the alignment of its satellite dish and that was easily fixed. Like the company itself, the brownstone was designed to last.

Nicholas swung into the private drive and moved past the valet station. The liveried attendant ran after the car as it pulled into one of the two dozen spaces—the one marked with a brass plaque that read *Nicholas Van Orton*. The valet opened the driver's side door.

"Good morning, Mr. Van Orton," the young man said as Nicholas reached over and grabbed his computer case.

"Good morning, Warner," Nicholas said formally. *And don't say it*, he thought. *Do not*.

"And a happy birthday, sir," the smiling attendant added. "With many happy returns."

Nicholas nodded unhappily. "Thank you very, very much," he said. He did not look back.

Then somehow everyone knew, dammit. He felt as if his privacy had been invaded and he hated that. Nicholas decided he'd add a "very" after each birthday wish. Make a sort of game of it.

If you can't beat it, you might as well spin it, he told himself. Have a little fun with it.

The door to the lobby was unlocked. The guard jumped from behind his desk and held it for him.

"Good morning, sir," said the middle-aged security officer, "and happy birthday."

"Thank you very, very, very much, Bicking," Nicholas replied coldly as he crossed the lobby. He walked quickly toward the winding staircase which led to his second-floor office.

He unlocked the door. His executive assistant, Maria Morris, didn't arrive until seven-thirty and the rest of his personal staff didn't get there until eight. He shut the door behind him, walked to his large desk—there was only a telephone on the marble surface—and opened his laptop. He jacked in and started downloading stock prices from Tokyo, London, and New York.

Happy birthday my frigging butt, he thought as he took off his Armani jacket and hung it on a hanger behind the door. Of course, it could have been worse. It could have been like that old 45 he listened to over and over when he was a kid. What were the words? *Another year older and deeper in debt?*

Yeah, things could be a whole lot worse, Nicholas Van Orton told himself as he carefully rolled up his shirtsleeves, sat down in his deep leather chair, and went to work.

chapter 3

Nicholas listened with half an ear to the cigarette raw voice coming from the phone.

". . . might be perched up on majority shares, but you're not the only one who gets hurt if the actuals crash."

"I hear you, Jack," Nicholas said. "But I don't want to do anything yet." He spoke firmly but quietly. One of the keys to power was to speak soft and make others listen hard. It forced them to shut up.

Everyone except Jack. The man was a brilliant broker who had been with Nicholas for years. But his in-your-face style—overcranked for the screamers and dense-heads in New York—annoyed the hell out of Nicholas. Nicholas rolled his eyes at Maria, who stood practically at attention in front of the desk. Her handsome face was impassive, her eyes peering straight ahead.

"Fine," Jack's voice continued. "I hear *you*. Just remember that the forecasts were seriously fucked to begin with—"

"I understand that," Nicholas said with a trace of impatience. He took a swallow of black coffee.

"Which is why you have to—"

"See Baer/Grant's P&L report," Nicholas cut in. "That's what I have to do. The moment it's placed in my hand I'll be speed-dialing your number so we can go over it."

There was a slight pause. "Is that a promise?" Jack asked.

"Sorry," Nicholas snickered. "I'm totally unfamiliar with that term."

If Jack got the joke, he didn't show it. "What if Anson calls me with a sob story about substantiation procedure?" he pressed.

"Then you do what you do when you play tag."

"Come again?"

"Tag," Nicholas said, raising his voice slightly. "The kid's game. You take evasive action. Have your secretary say you're in a meeting. I mean really, Jack. You know the drill."

"Knowing it and liking it are two different things."

"Not if you want to play in my game," Nicholas said. "Now good-bye."

"Okay," Jack said. "'Bye."

Nicholas hung up. "Je-*sus*," he said. At least the bastard hadn't wished him a happy birthday. He still wondered how those other people knew. Nicholas looked at the computer and began shuffling through the latest pie charts from his friends at YunfatCo in Hong Kong.

"So now, Maria," he said without looking up, "what world-shaking social matters have you got for me?"

Maria glanced down at an index card. "First, invitations to the art museum gala."

"No. You like that crap. You take them."

"How about the Fitzwilliam Botanical Annual Fund-raiser."

"God, no. Send a check, decline the nondeductible bullshit, and give the tickets to the janitor."

"The Hinchberger wedding."

"Aw, jeez, Maria, what the hell's wrong with you?" Nicholas said disgustedly. He sat back and touched his temples. "Let me think. Hordes of men in tuxedos. Every-one droning in my ear about investing in this cousin's business or that brother-in-law's invention. The always embarrassing Ludwell trying to break the ice that always seems to surround him by reciting off-color limericks." He glared at her. "Beautiful young women wanting me to dance with them because they're in their twenties, single, and want a rich guy to take to the cleaners. "

"I'll send your regrets," Maria said tensely. "Honestly, I don't see why I bother responding at all. If you just ignore the invitations, maybe people will stop sending them."

"Ah, but that isn't how it works," Nicholas said. "You see, one of the deep satisfactions that comes from being a part of society is avoiding it. Nothing offends them more than saying, 'Nah . . . I don't wanna come to your god-damn party.' Understand?"

She nodded. She probably did. She'd once been one of those twentysomethings who'd tried to woo him. He half-suspected that she went to work for him years before to show that she could stand him day after day. Now she earned too much to afford to go anywhere else.

There was a knock on the door.

"Come!" Nicholas said.

A young female assistant entered, along with a wave of noise and activity behind her. "Mr. Van Orton?"

"Yes, Maggie?"

"Elizabeth on line three."

Nicholas was still sitting back in his chair. The leather squeaked as he shifted uncomfortably.

"Your ex-wife," Maria said.

"I know who she is," Nicholas said. "And Maria—for the millionth time it's *former* wife. 'Ex-' makes it sound like she's dead." He glanced over at the eager, attractive Maggie. "Take a message."

"Yes, sir," she smiled. "And—happy birthday, sir."

Nicholas flashed a big, fake smile. "Thank you very, very, very, very, very much."

Maggie backed out and shut the door. When it was closed, Maria looked at Nicholas. "What was that all about?"

"What?"

"Those verys."

"Oh, just a little game I'm playing with myself. A very little game, you might say." He steepled his hands in front of his chin. "Tell me. How did everyone know it was my birthday, anyway?"

"Probably from the newspaper," Maria replied. "I'm guessing you're in that new 'Milestones of Notable San Franciscans' column."

"Oh, fuck them!" Nicholas said disgustedly. "Check it out. If I am in there, call Barry Neville and tell him if he ever runs a personal notice about me again I'll buy his goddamn paper and seriously fire his ass."

Maria made a note on her index cards. "I'll tell him in exactly those words," she said.

"That's what I pay you to do," Nicholas said. "And since by the tone of your voice I gather you don't approve—because Barry's a terribly sweet guy, wouldn't hurt a mosquito—let me remind you that equivocators never prosper. If you're going to do something, do it with all your weapons." He returned to his computer. He'd lost fifty thousand dollars on Biggs Entertainment while he was sitting here chatting. "Anything else?"

"Just one thing. I wouldn't mention it except that he was very insistent."

"Who was?"

"It's obviously some sort of prank."

"*What* is?" Nicholas demanded.

"Well, a gentleman called earlier requesting a lunch. I assured him—"

"For the last time—what gentleman, Maria?"

"A Mr. Butts," she said. "Seymour Butts."

Nicholas looked up. A smile pulled at one end of his mouth. His eyes drifted down until they were looking straight ahead—and back through the years.

Under the Bleachers," he said to himself.

"Pardon me?" Maria said. "I'm afraid I don't—"

"*Under the Bleachers* by Seymour Butts,'" Nicholas said. He smiled openly now. "A fake book title, like *The Yellow River* by I. P. Daley or *The Hernia* by Won Hung Lo. Maria, cancel lunch."

"But your attorney has papers for you to—"

"Make reservations at City Club for me and Mr. Butts. Make sure I get my table. As for Attorney Marley, tell her she can haul her ass over here this afternoon and I'll sign the papers then. She's sharper when she hasn't had anything to drink anyway."

Maria nodded as she made notes on her index card. Then she turned and walked toward the door, her high heels clicking on the hardwood floor.

"Maria?"

She stopped and turned completely around. "Yes?"

"On second thought, just put the reservation in my name."

Maria nodded again, turned, and left the office.

Nicholas was still smiling as the door closed with a loud click.

chapter 4

The morning passed quickly. It always did for Nicholas. It was only when you had time to stop and look at your watch that time went slowly.

Nicholas's reservation was for 12:30. He left the office at 12:15 and arrived at the City Club in Seacliff at 12:25. The restaurant at the private club had a view of the ocean on one side and the city on the other. Nicholas's table faced the water. When he'd first started coming here in the early 1980s, he liked the idea of being able to "look out" at Japan, to see the face of what was then the enemy. As if he could will them bad luck across almost nine thousand miles of ocean.

Well, maybe it had worked after all, he thought as he took his seat. He put his napkin on his lap, ordered an iced tea, set the menu aside, and began looking at a thick stack of financial statements. "Mr. Butts" was usually prompt, but Nicholas hated even five minutes of downtime. Time was money and money was power and power was everything. There were times when he'd considered running for public office. He certainly had the cash and the connections and a clean enough history.

His iced tea arrived. He drink thirstily as he reviewed the statements—and, on the occasion of his birthday, continued to review the course his life had taken.

Even as governor or president he would have had to make compromises. Work with a legislature or cabinet or counterparts overseas. As the head of the Van Orton Group, his word was law.

The waitress returned. "Are you ready to order, sir?"

"No," he said. "I'm waiting for someone. Or didn't you notice the other plate?"

"I'm sorry, sir," she said. She turned to go.

"Excuse me, miss?"

"Yes, sir?"

He pushed the empty glass toward her with a finger. "This was iced tea"—he glanced at her name tag—"Christine."

"I'm sorry, sir," she said, with a slightly irritated smile. "Just let me get the pitcher and I'll refill it."

"Do that. And go lighter on the ice."

"Of course, sir."

"I mean your attitude, Christine," he said. "Not the drink."

She glared at him then left silently.

Nicholas returned to his statements. If that girl had worked for him, she wouldn't. He didn't care about unions and employee organizations and government watchdog groups or any of that. If people did their jobs well, they were rewarded. If they didn't, they were shit-canned. He'd spent hundreds of thousands of dollars fighting wrongful dismissal suits. It was a matter of principle and it was tax deductible so why the hell not?

Nicholas checked his watch. It was 12:33. He sighed. A moment later someone sneezed directly behind him. The spray hit his neck.

"Son of a *shit*!" Nicholas yelled, drawing stares from other diners. He jumped up from his chair and turned.

And looked at a young man holding an atomizer and

wearing a crooked little smile. He stood five-nine, two inches shorter than Nicholas, but he had broader shoulders and a thicker, once athletic build. He had short black hair and a round face—his mother's face. His nose was highly arched, the result of repeated breaks suffered in high school football. That was when he still cared about his body . . . and still had the drive to stick with something despite setbacks.

"Happy birthday, Nickie," Conrad said.

Nicholas used his napkin to wipe the water from the back of his neck.

The waitress arrived with the pitcher of iced tea.

"Ooo, that looks—boring," Conrad said. "Could I have a Bloody Mary please?"

The waitress asked, "Are you asking me, sir, or the other gentleman?"

"Ah," said Conrad, "I see you two have met. You, ma'am. Please."

"I'll get it right away," she said.

Nicholas ignored the woman's sass. For now. He'd E-mail the executive president about her when he got back to the office.

Nicholas shook his head. " 'Seymour Butts,' " he said. "I must admit, Conrad, I'll never get tired of that one."

"I know," he grinned. "It's a classic."

Conrad took a step forward and hugged his brother tightly. Nicholas put his arms stiffly around the younger man's shoulders. Nicholas broke first and took his seat. Conrad dragged the chair out loudly and plopped into it.

"Nice restaurant," he said. He ran his thumbs under the lapels of his tan blazer. "They gave me a free jacket."

"They'll be wanting it back," Nicholas said.

"Yeah, well, I already got one at home. Not this color— navy blue. But who needs two sports coats anyway?"

"Not you," Nicholas said.

Conrad looked around, nodding. "Y'know, I remember being here a long time ago."

"I know," Nicholas said. "I took you."

"Nah, I'm not talkin' about then," Conrad said. "I mean alone. I once bought crystal meth from the maître d'."

"Really? When?"

"In college."

"Which college?" Nicholas asked. "The one you dropped out of, the one you got thrown out of, or the one where you managed to do each of those once?"

"Touché," Conrad grinned.

Conrad's drink arrived and the waitress asked if they'd like to hear the specials. Nicholas told her to come back in five minutes. He stared at his brother.

"So," Conrad said as he took a sip. "Miss me?"

"As much as that's possible," he said. "Actually, you look good."

"So do you. And to think I was worried."

"About me? You were worried—about me?"

Conrad reached into his shirt pocket. "Yeah."

Nicholas snickered.

"How long's it been?" Conrad asked. "Since Mom's funeral? Two, two-and-a-half years?"

Nicholas nodded.

"Time flies," Conrad said as he plucked a cigarette from his pocket.

"I thought you quit," Nicholas said.

"I did." He put the cigarette in his mouth and bent toward the candle on the table. "It didn't take."

"Well, you can't smoke here," Nicholas said.

"Why not? I'm with you. I'm with Mr. Big."

"Doesn't matter. You can't smoke in any restaurant in California. It's illegal."

"Fuck California," Conrad said.

"I have," Nicholas said. "Repeatedly. But you still can't smoke in here."

Conrad sat up. He tucked the unlit cigarette back into his pocket. "No big whoop," he said. "I just quit. I'll start up again later." He regarded his brother. "So how are you?"

"Never better."

"Elizabeth?"

"We're divorced," Nicholas said. "She's remarried to some pediatrician or gynecologist or pediatric gynecologist. They live in Sausalito."

"That's too bad," Conrad said. "I liked her."

"Me too," Nicholas said.

"Are you all alone in the House of Pain?"

"Women come and go," he said. "And Ilsa's still there."

"Poor McIver's favorite Teuton," Conrad said.

"She's good, hardworking people," Nicholas said. "What about you? Where are you living?"

"Here and there," he said. "I send changes-of-address to your office. Don't you keep track of me anymore?"

"I gave up following your migrations after the last family week at rehab."

Conrad looked down. "Memo to Nickie: not everyone's an overachiever. And not everyone can handle living in the shadow of an overachiever."

Nicholas took a long sip of iced tea. He looked at his brother's downturned face and he thought about the joyful, frolicking kid he'd seen in the movies the night before. Nicholas felt a rush of compassion, though he reminded himself that Conrad was a fuckup. He was a good-natured guy, but a fuckup all the same. And people like that just couldn't change what they were.

"What brings you here, Connie?" Nicholas asked. His voice was soft—brotherly. "Is everything all right?"

He rolled a shoulder. "Sure." He still didn't look up.

"You need anything?" Nicholas asked.

Conrad shook his head.

"You sure?"

"I'm sure," Conrad said. He regarded his brother. "I'm

here because I was lying naked on a beach near Havana and it hits me—October 12th. That's Nickie's birthday."

"October 11th."

"What-the-fuck-ever. So here I am, one donkey ride and four layovers later. Not necessarily in that order." He reached around and pulled an envelope from his back pants pocket. "Here. For you."

Nicholas picked up the oversized envelope. He slid a finger under the flap. "You shouldn't have."

"You know me, Nickie. If I've got it, I'll spend it. That's why I ain't 'got' much of it."

Nicholas pulled out the birthday card. There was a photograph of a birthday cake. He opened it and a business card slipped out. Nicholas picked it up from the table. It said *Consumer Recreation Services*. There was a phone number and an address below it. No fax or website. He looked at the birthday card. There was nothing written inside.

"Hey, Connie, thanks," Nicholas said. "But I already have golf clubs and a squash racquet."

"Call that number," Connie said.

The glibness was gone from Conrad's voice. Nicholas's eyes narrowed. He drained his iced tea as he looked at his brother. "Why should I call?" he asked. He put the glass down.

"Because they make your life fun."

"Fun?"

"You've heard of that," Conrad said. "You've seen other people having it."

"Come on, Connie. Cut the sarcasm—"

"Sure, big brother. Anything you say. What they are is an entertainment service."

"You mean an escort service?"

"I mean a profound life experience," Conrad replied.

Christine returned with the pitcher of iced tea. She began pouring. And pouring. The glass overflowed.

"Watch what the hell you're doing!" Nicholas snapped.

26

He drew his napkin from his lap and threw it on the pool of liquid as it rolled toward the edge of the table.

"Oh, I'm so very, very sorry!" Christine said. "Let me get you another napkin."

"In a minute," he said. "If we could just order first—"

Christine had already moved off. She disappeared behind a door. Nicholas looked with exasperation at his brother.

"Can you beat this shit?" Nicholas said.

Conrad shrugged. "I've seen worse." He turned a thumb toward the card. "Tell me you'll call."

"I said I would."

"No, you didn't. You asked, 'Why should I?' "

"Fine," Nicholas said. "I'll call." He regarded his brother for a moment. "Are you still on medication?"

Conrad seemed perplexed. "Why? Why would you ask me that?"

"Because you seem unusually calm."

"I do?"

"Yeah."

"Well, maybe that's because we haven't seen each other in over two years. This is me—the *new* me. Or maybe you're just unusually hyper."

Nicholas pushed the wet napkin aside. "Cool it, Connie. Don't get pissy with me."

"Why not? Hey, aren't I the chronic loser who can't hold a conversation without saying something inappropriate or making a spectacle of himself?"

"It's been known to happen," Nicholas said.

Conrad's shoulders slumped. He exhaled loudly and shook his head. "I can't ever win with you, can I?"

"Don't talk like that," Nicholas said. "Look, I didn't mean this like it sounded. I'm sorry. It *is* good to see you."

Conrad leaned forward on the table and regarded his brother. "If you really want to know how I am, I'm fine. I'm not on anything anymore. I'm not even seeing a shrink. I feel great."

The waitress returned then. She didn't have the extra napkin. "Are you gentlemen ready to order?"

"Not yet," Conrad said. He looked at her. "How about I bang the glass with my fork when I'm ready?" he said, slightly irate.

"Or you can use the candle to send smoke signals," she said cheerfully. She turned and left.

"*I* can't!" Nicholas said, yelling after her. "My napkin's all fucking wet!"

The waitress disappeared again.

Conrad continued to regard his brother. He chucked his chin toward the business card. "Anyway—I thought you'd like this. I did. It was the best thing that ever happened to me."

Nicholas turned back to his brother. "I'll call them, okay?"

"Don't do it for me," Conrad said. "Do it for you."

"I'm going to call them for me. O-fucking-kay?"

Conrad nodded.

Nicholas glanced down at the card. "Entertainment. Christ, Connie. I just—you know I hate surprises."

"I know," he said, picking up his salad fork. He clinked it twice against his water glass.

As Conrad smiled wryly, waiters, waitresses, and bus-boys came through the door through which Christine had vanished. They were all singing "Happy Birthday" and carrying a small cake with a lighted candle.

Nicholas glared at his brother. Conrad rose and joined in with the singing. So did the other patrons in the dining room.

"I'll kill you later," Nicholas said through his teeth as the cake was placed before him.

For now, though, he forced a tight smile and let his brother have fun at his expense. He'd let him play his little game. . . .

chapter 5

The morning drive was a time when Nicholas enjoyed racing the engine and listening to fast classical music. It always jump-started his personal engine, psyched him up for the daily hunt. In contrast, the evening commute was simply an extension of the business day. It was a time for driving slow and working the cellular phone. It was quiet Chopin Nocturnes now, not Etudes, that drifted from the car's four speakers.

The sun added its own subdued heat to the dying day. It threw a deep orange light on the old Victorian homes that lined the street. Now and then the row of stately facades was broken by glassy, high-rise condos; they spoiled the charm of the expensive neighborhood and its million-dollar-plus estates, but they offered an unparalleled view of the Bay and the city.

Nicholas listened as Emiko Kochi gave him the morning rundown from Tokyo.

". . . seen the profitability report. No one here or in Hong Kong is happy with those numbers."

"Imagine how much *more* unhappy I am. My wallet's the one that's hemorrhaging."

"As far as I can see, Nicholas, there's just one way out." Nicholas's jaw tightened. "Agreed."

"Then—you'll deal with Anson?"

"Correct." The word nearly snagged in his throat.

"Fine," Emiko said. "I'll try to make it as painless as possible."

"That's why you and I are in business, Emi."

"Is it? And for all these years I thought it was just because you liked bilingual women."

"That too," Nicholas said. "I'll talk to you tomorrow."

"Okay, Nicholas. Sleep well."

"I intend to," he said.

Nicholas disconnected the phone. He dropped it on the passenger's seat. He turned up the volume on the CD player. Opus 9, Number 2 was playing. The nocturne was Nicholas's favorite. It was pianist Eddy Duchin's signature piece. Nicholas's mother had one of his recordings of the nocturne and she used to play it all the time. More than any other piece of music, hearing this one brought him back to his childhood—

He turned to his left, toward the Queen Annes and English Tudors, which rolled past. Most were restored, some were survivors of the 1906 earthquake and fire.

Survivors, he thought. He liked the sound of that word.

Nicholas vividly remembered driving these same streets on a particular day in 1959. He was ten years old and sitting quietly in the back of the family station wagon, behind the chauffeur. His briefcase crammed with schoolbooks was sitting beside him. Conrad was rolling around in the back of the car, pretending that he was on a raft in the middle of the ocean.

The Van Orton mansion loomed ahead now, just as it had then. There was a keypad beside the CD player of the BMW. Nicholas input the code VEEB, Victorian Elegance Every Block—he never used PINs like VANO or 1949, which someone might guess—and the gate began to open. As he waited, he frowned. He remembered . . .

When there was no gate. He remembered the sense of well-being he always felt when the station wagon swung around the brick columns at the end of the driveway and the house came into view. The driver would always wish him and his brother a cheerful good afternoon and then they would bound from the car. Only once did Nicholas come home and feel cold inside. It was on that day in 1959. *This* day. His tenth birthday. As the boys ran past the rosebushes that lined the driveway, Conrad stopped to climb a tree—it was the mast of his raft, he said—and Nicholas continued toward the house. Looking up, he saw his father standing on the edge of the rooftop. He was wearing his blue bathrobe and staring at the sky.

Nicholas stopped slowly. He waved tentatively at his father. The older Van Orton did not acknowledge him. He just stared up, his expression blank. Nicholas, too, stared up, his expression blank. . . .

The gate opened. Nicholas shifted gears, pressed his foot to the pedal, and eased along the driveway.

Ilsa was just coming through the kitchen door. Behind her, about two hundred yards away, was the guest house in which she'd lived for nearly forty-nine years. She stopped and waited while Nicholas parked and got out of the car.

"Dinner's in the oven," she said as he approached the garden.

"Thank you. Good night."

"Good night," she said. She turned to go.

Nicholas reached the sliding glass door. He stopped. "I saw Conrad this afternoon," he said.

Ilsa stopped about ten yards away. She turned, her features lost in the shadows of twilight. "Did you? How is he?"

"Good, I guess. I think he's into some sort of new personal improvement regimen."

Ilsa seemed a little uncomfortable. "That's nice," she said. She had always liked Conrad. Favored him, really. Ilsa was serious, Conrad was fun, and opposites do attract. "If you see him again, send my love."

"I took that liberty," Nicholas said.

"Thank you," she said. "Well good night again. And happy birthday."

Nicholas nodded and Ilsa left.

He stood alone in the dark for several seconds. It was the first quiet he'd experienced since morning. It felt good.

chapter 6

Nicholas pulled on a pair of mitts and removed his dinner plate from the oven. He set it on a waiting tray beside a champagne flute and a cupcake with a birthday candle stuck in the chocolate icing. The huge cheeseburger and crispy, hand-cut french fries were hot and perfectly presented. This was the way to end a long day. He carried the tray into the cavernous library.

The champagne bucket was waiting beside his deep-cushioned recliner. He put the tray on a mahogany table beside the chair, setting it in its spot between the telephone and the three remote controls—one for the TV, one for the VCR, and one for the digital video disc player. He sat, picked up the TV remote control, and pointed it at the forty-two-inch direct-view TV in the corner. CNN popped on. He spread the cloth napkin on his lap and ate his dinner as he waited for the financial news. Then he opened the champagne bottle and poured. He toasted no one as he took a sip and set the glass back down. He shut his eyes.

He jumped as the phone rang. He looked at his watch. It was 11:40. He'd been asleep for over four hours. He hit the mute button on the remote then pushed the speakerphone button.

"Hello?" he said groggily.

"Happy birthday, Nick."

Nicholas sat up. "Elizabeth. Hi." He took a swallow of warm champagne to wash out his mouth. "How are you?"

"Fine. Did you have a great birthday?"

"Did Rose Kennedy have a black dress? I got put through the spanking machine today. By Connie."

"Connie?" she said. "I always liked him."

"I know. So. You managed to catch me this year."

"I had to," she said. "I thought this one might be difficult for you."

"Just another birthday," he replied. He took another sip of champagne. *Why am I bullshitting her?* he asked himself. *We're not married anymore.*

"I see," she said. "I thought today might be different— because of your father."

"Hadn't thought about that," he lied. The elder Van Orton was forty-eight when he did it. When he spread his arms on the rooftop that day, bent his knees deeply, and launched himself into space. Toward his son. Nicholas had watched in silence, turning away only after his father struck loudly the stone path less than two yards from where he stood. Behind him, Conrad had screamed from the top of the tree, *Daaaaddy!* "But you're right," Nicholas said. "Pop *was* forty-eight, wasn't he? Wow. Thanks for the reminder, Elizabeth. Maybe we can start an office pool. 'Will Nicholas Van Orton leap from the top of the Van Orton Group building before he turns forty-nine?'"

"Nick, cut it out."

"No, really. We can announce it in the paper. Get the whole city in on it."

"Why do I bother calling you?" Elizabeth said with disgust.

"I honestly don't know, Liz. Listen, I gotta go. Give my best to Doctor Mel and to Rachel."

"She has a little brother on the way. We just did the ultrasound."

"An official nuclear family," Nicholas said. "You must be very pleased."

"We are."

Nicholas smiled thinly. He meant that *she* must be very pleased. Elizabeth knew it and went out of her way to play the family card on him. The card that he never wanted in his hand.

"Well, so . . . ," he said. "Thank you for calling."

"Right. It's late. I should let you go."

"Take care of yourself."

"You, too, Nicholas. I mean that. I really do."

"Uh-huh. Good luck with the baby. Bye."

He cut off the speakerphone in the middle of Elizabeth's "good-bye." He unmuted the TV. He rubbed his eyes, undid his tie, and felt the business card in his shirt pocket. The one Conrad had given him. He took it out and looked at it.

Consumer Recreation Services.

They make your life fun, Conrad had said. *A profound life experience. The best thing that ever happened to me.*

Nicholas stared up at the vaulted ceiling. Conrad had always lived life on the edge, whether he was climbing a tree or getting himself into Cuba. When he started using words like "profound" and "best," you could take that to the bank.

"All right, Connie," Nicholas said. "I'm game." He rose from the chair, flicked the card with his thumb and middle finger, made a mental note to call in the morning.

chapter 7

Nicholas didn't call.

The next morning he played squash with two of his partners in a complex leveraged buyout. They began talking business in the steam room, continued as they walked along Fifth Street, and didn't quite finish until they were in the elevator at his partners' office building. Nicholas got off with the two men at their twenty-first-floor suite.

"So we understand each other?" Nicholas said in a low voice as they walked away from the elevator.

"We do," said one.

"Make it work on paper and you can count on my full support."

"Right-o," said the same man. "We'll talk. Soon."

The men shook hands and the two executives continued down the corridor. Nicholas turned and walked back to the elevator. He pushed the button. As he waited, he happened to turn around. Behind him was a translucent glass wall on which the initials CRS were written large in bold, gold letters.

"No," he said. "It couldn't be."

He stepped forward and peered through the glass. A

receptionist sat at a glass-topped desk and was speaking into a headset phone. Employees moved around the cubicles behind her. Electricians and telephone installers worked in and around the crawl space behind a water cooler.

Nicholas took the business card from his wallet. "I'll be damned," he said. This was the address. This had to be Consumer Recreation Services.

Nicholas looked at his watch. He didn't really have the time for this. But, *What the hell?* he thought. He was here.

He pushed open the door and walked over to the desk.

". . . you shouldn't feel this reflects negatively on you," the young and beautiful receptionist was saying into the phone.

Nicholas showed the receptionist the card. "Is this Consumer Recreation Services?"

She looked up at him with clear blue eyes. "Just a moment," she whispered to Nicholas as she took the card. She smiled then turned back to the phone. "We hope we haven't caused you any inconvenience," she said. "Thank you for considering C.R.S." She clicked off and turned halfway around. "Mr. Feingold?" she said. "Could you assist this gentleman?"

Behind her, a balding, middle-aged man was paying a delivery boy from the New Moon Cafe. When the youth left, Feingold walked over. He took the card from the receptionist, tucked it in the hand holding the food bag, and extended his free hand.

"Hi. Jim Feingold, VP, Engineering and Data Analysis."

"Hello," Nicholas said formally. "Nicholas Van Orton. Mr. Feingold, I'm not quite sure what this is or how it works. My brother—"

"Hold that thought," Feingold said as he turned over the card. "Ah—it's all here."

"What is?" Nicholas asked. His palm felt clammy under the handle of his briefcase. He hoped those utility guys were fixing the air-conditioning. It was warm in here.

Feingold pointed to the back of the card. There were four numbers printed along one edge. "This is all we need to get started." He held his arm toward a corridor. "Would you follow me, Mr. Van Orton?"

"To tell you the truth, Mr. Feingold, I'm not sure if I have the time for this now."

Feingold smiled and walked ahead. Nicholas looked at the receptionist, who had already taken another call. He sighed and thought again, *What the hell?* He was here.

He took a deep breath and followed Feingold.

There were at least two dozen cubicles lining the corridor. Clean-cut employees, all in white shirts or blouses with black pants or skirts, were coming and going from them. Most of them were in a hurry. Nicholas saw a few stony-faced customers sitting in chairs beside the utilitarian desks.

He thought *What the hell?* again, only this time it was as in *What the hell am I doing here?*

"Sorry about all the hullabaloo," Feingold said over his shoulder, the bag of food swinging at his side. "We're still moving."

"I noticed."

"I've got an office around here somewhere—ah! Here we are."

He stopped beside the last cubicle. There were two open boxes on either side of the doorless doorway. They were stuffed with papers and folders.

Feingold handed Nicholas the bag of Chinese food. "Would you mind holding this?" he asked.

Nicholas made a face as he accepted the greasy bag.

"If you're hungry, Mr. Van Orton, feel free to dig right in. I always order too much anyway."

"No, thank you," Nicholas replied.

"You sure? New Moon Cafe. Best in Chinatown."

"I'll let you know if I change my mind," Nicholas said. He looked at the menu stapled to the bag. There was a large, grinning cartoon dragon on top. It reminded him of Cecil the Seasick Sea Serpent, whose cartoons he and Conrad used to watch when they were kids. That was fitting, Nicholas thought, because Feingold reminded him of Cecil's partner Beany. Nicholas's eyes drifted over to the VP, Engineering and Data Analysis. He was pulling forms from various folders. "Is this going to take a lot of time?" Nicholas asked impatiently.

"Not at all," he said. He stood proudly and smiled. "I've got all the documents I need. Won't you come in?"

Feingold went inside. He placed the documents beside the computer on his desk then reached out and took the bag from Nicholas. Feingold held a hand toward a chair beside the desk. Nicholas sat reluctantly.

Feingold opened the bag, pulled out a carton of pork lo mein, and unwrapped the chopsticks. Nicholas noticed the same stylized dragon cartoon on the container. *Good for the New Moon Cafe*, Nicholas thought: even small business-people needed to understand the importance of brand recognition.

Feingold pulled open the overstuffed carton. "Ever since I've been using chopsticks," he said, "which is about ten years now, I feel like I should eat everything that way. Pretty weird, huh?"

"Insanely."

"Of course, maybe that's because just about all I eat is Chinese food," Feingold said.

Nicholas looked at his watch. "Mr. Feingold, can we get on with this?"

"Mmmm, of course," he said as he bent low over the container and pushed noodles into his mouth. He sat up, jabbed the chopsticks back into the lo mein, and turned to the keyboard. "Let's see now," he said, chewing. "That was V-a-n . . . O-r-t-o-n. Correct?"

Nicholas nodded.

"Excellent. Now we just . . ." Feingold's voice trailed

off as he punched in the numbers from the back of the card. He pressed enter, sat back, and watched as a file appeared on-screen. "I see this is a gift from Conrad Van Orton."

"That's right," said Nicholas.

"Hmm. This is interesting."

"What is?"

Feingold plucked a piece of pork from the carton and popped it in his mouth. He chewed loudly. "Your brother was a client of our London branch."

"Why is that interesting?"

"Oh no, not that," Feingold said. "See, we do a sort of informal scoring. His numbers were outstanding."

"His numbers?"

"Mmm, yes," Feingold said. He pushed the carton toward Nicholas while he continued to study the screen. "Sure you're not hungry?"

"I'm very sure. I don't follow. What numbers were outstanding?"

"Your brother's," Feingold said, as though the answer were self-evident.

Nicholas experienced the momentary sensation of having slipped down Alice's rabbit hole.

"Okay," Feingold said. "Before we go any further you need to fill out these." He handed Nicholas the thin stack of papers he'd pulled from the box. "You have a pen?"

"Yes," Nicholas said. He looked at the top form as he popped his briefcase and withdrew his fountain pen. "What exactly am I filling out?"

"An application, psych tests: MMPI and TAT. For the financial questionnaire, don't answer anything you don't feel like."

"I won't—"

"We'll be running a TRW in any case."

I've definitely gone down the rabbit hole, Nicholas thought. This entire process was so bizarre, so surreal he had to follow it to see where it went. He shut his briefcase, set it flat on his lap, and lay the forms on top of it. He filled out the personal data on top—name, address, phone numbers, age, marital status—then read the first question aloud.

"'I sometimes hurt small animals, true or false.'" He looked at Feingold, who was scrolling through the on-screen file and eating his lo mein. "What is this?"

Feingold looked over. "The first page of the psych profile."

Nicholas glanced down. He read the second question. "'I feel guilty when I masturbate'—What kind of crap is this?"

Feingold shrugged, embarrassed. "I don't write the questions. I just review them."

"For what?"

"To get a sense of a prospective client's overall capabilities, limitations, turn-ons, turn-offs."

"Yes, but what's all this *for*? What are you people selling?"

Feingold seemed surprised. "Don't you know?"

"Would I ask if I did?"

"I guess not," said Feingold. "I'm sorry. I thought you knew." He pushed his lunch aside, folded his soft hands on the desk, and assumed a more professional demeanor. If he'd had a bad toupee, Nicholas thought, Feingold would have been the very model of a low-rent insurance salesman. "What we're selling, Mr. Van Orton, is . . . a game."

"A game?"

"Yes. One which is tailored to each participant. Think of it as a great vacation except you don't go to it. It comes to you."

"I don't understand. What comes to me?"

"It's different every time."

"Humor me with specifics," Nicholas pressed.

"We provide whatever's lacking."

"And if nothing's lacking?"

Feingold grinned and looked at him: *as if.*

"I mean," Nicholas continued, "you clowns think I'll participate in something without knowing *anything*?"

Feingold was still grinning. "May I make two suggestions?"

"Only if at least one of them contains the words 'Good afternoon, Mr. Van Orton.'" Nicholas replaced his pen, put the papers on the desk, and rose. "Good afternoon, Mr. Feingold."

"Mr. Van Orton," Feingold said, "you're an extremely successful businessperson."

"That's right," Nicholas said. He started to turn away. "And I didn't get that way by leaping without looking."

"Exactly," Feingold said. "You take deals one step at a time. Mr. Van Orton: that's what I'd like you to do here."

Nicholas stopped. He turned back toward Feingold. The grin had faded and the eyes were suddenly, surprisingly, sincere.

"All right," Nicholas said. "I'll bite. What are your two suggestions?"

"First," Feingold said, "I hope you'll admit—to yourself, at least—that this all sounds intriguing. Second, I want you to keep in mind that you don't have to decide anything today. Take the silly tests, fill out the stupid forms, answer the dumb questions. Then, one day, the game begins. You either love it or you hate it. We're like an experiential Book-of-the-Month Club. Drop out anytime you wish, with no further obligation." He smiled again, this time warmly. The eyes softened. "That was my sales pitch. Good afternoon, Mr. Van Orton. Or . . . ?"

The VP, Engineering and Data Analysis, picked up a ballpoint pen, clicked it, and offered it to Nicholas.

Nicholas noticed the tiny C.R.S. letters in gold on the side of the green barrel. His eyes shifted to the papers on the desk. He glanced at his watch. "How long will these take?"

"An hour for the forms, tops. Maybe another hour for the physical."

"Physical?"

"A cursory examination," Feingold said. "Turn-your-head-and-cough sort of thing. You'll be out of here in no time."

Nicholas looked at Feingold. He sighed again and accepted the pen. He sat down.

"Thank you," Feingold said.

Nicholas pulled the papers back onto his briefcase. He read aloud as he began checking off boxes.

" 'I often feel someone is following me, true or false. I hate vegetables, true or false. Vegetables hate me, true or false.' "

To his left, Mr. Feingold resumed eating his Chinese food and studying his computer monitor. He'd been wrong about one thing. Nicholas didn't find "this all" intriguing. What interested him was his own willingness to participate in such an intrusive process. And it occurred to him, as he went through the forms, that maybe what he was doing was trying to show Conrad something. Maybe call his bluff. Maybe prove that Conrad wasn't the only one who dared to climb a tree or sail the South Pacific or live for the day.

Maybe he wanted to show Conrad that Nicholas Van Orton had balls.

And—okay, Mr. Feingold—maybe he also wanted to prove that to Nicholas Van Orton.

chapter 8

Nicholas spent less than an hour on the paperwork but more than an hour on the rest of the "induction," as he came to regard it.

The induction consisted of more than just the "cough," as Feingold had glibly put it. There was that, of course. But then Nicholas was asked to put on earphones and listen to high-pitched beeps. He was to raise a finger from his left hand for every low beep, a finger on his right hand for every high beep. The beeps came through different earphones in no discernible pattern—sometimes two highs from the right followed by one low from the right, and then a high-low from the left. He presumed that this was to test his ability to keep his left and right hands straight when his ears were being misled.

After that, Nicholas was told (no longer asked) to put on a paper gown and was shown to a laboratory. There he was hooked to sensors and wires, his heart and brain waves displayed on electronic monitors and printers. He put up with the indignities not only because he was in this far, but also because he was curious to see just how far it would go. He did, however, ask for a telephone. The young nurse brought one over and then proceeded to attach a blood pressure cuff to Nicholas's arm. While she worked, Nicholas punched in Maria's direct line.

"Nicholas!" she said. "Where have you been?"

"Tied up unexpectedly," he said as he looked over at the cuff. "I want you to cancel whatever I have left for the morning and push it over to Wednesday. What else has been happening?"

"Mr. Sutherland called about Baer/Grant Publishing," she said. "He said it's urgent that you—"

"Tomorrow," Nicholas said. "Hold on, Maria." He turned to the nurse. "How much longer is this going to take?"

"We're almost done," she said.

"We were almost done two hours ago," he replied.

She smiled pleasantly.

Following the physical examination, Nicholas was shown to a small white room where he was given a string of psychological tests by a grim-faced psychologist in a white lab coat. Her name tag said *Heather Jackson*.

Ms. Jackson showed him flash cards with simple cartoon drawings. He was instructed to give his reaction to each picture. His responses were recorded.

Ms. Jackson held up a picture with a large ant in an apron feeding a TV dinner to a human child.

"Dinner with Aunt Rose," Nicholas replied.

Ms. Jackson made no response to the comment. She held up a picture of a man slipping on a banana peel.

"A nice fall day," he said.

The psychologist held up a picture of a serpent.

"The logo for a new Chinese restaurant," Nicholas said. "And Ms. Jackson—I've got to get to a bathroom."

Ms. Jackson pointed to a door in the hallway. When he returned, she was ready with a new set of images. She'd pulled over an armchair with a set of buttons on the right armrest.

"Push the buttons to express your reaction," she said.

"The blue button for 'pleasant,' the yellow button for 'neutral,' and the red button for 'unpleasant.'"

He pressed red before the pictures began. She scowled at him.

The room was darkened and the pictures were projected from a computer monitor on a table behind him onto a screen on the wall in front.

For a moment Nicholas felt as if he were back in his den, watching home movies. Only these weren't pictures of the Van Orton family. They were pictures of U.S. Presidents, of insects devouring other insects, of car crashes, sunny beaches, busy city streets, sporting events, combat, and old age homes. There were mountains, graves, and puppies. They appeared one every three seconds. He knew because he counted.

After what felt like ten minutes, Nicholas stopped pushing the buttons. He turned and gazed into the bright glow behind him.

"I think I've had enough of this," he said.

No one answered.

He shielded his eyes with his hand and squinted into the light. "Ms. Jackson? Heather?"

There was still no answer.

Nicholas rose. "Hello!" he yelled. "Is anyone there?"

The lights came on and the computer went off. Nicholas winced from the sudden brightness. There was no one else in the room. For the first time he noticed, above and behind him, a small mirrored dome. Obviously a camera. He frowned and started toward the door. Just as he was about to reach for the knob, Mr. Feingold walked in. He was carrying Nicholas's briefcase.

"You left this in the examination room," Feingold said. "Sorry to have kept you waiting."

Nicholas grabbed his briefcase. "Hey, don't worry," he snapped. "It's been terrific spending the entire day with your 'crack team.' I feel like I'm ready for the army now."

"Our people are really very good, Mr. Van Orton. They do everything that's necessary to ensure the safety and satisfaction of our clients."

"I'm sure. Look, Mr. Feingold, it's been a shitload of fun but now I've really got to—"

"Go, yes, I know," Feingold said. He held up a Lucite clipboard. "Just one more thing."

Nicholas made a face. "No. No more things."

"Mr. Van Orton, you've stayed with us until now," Feingold said sheepishly. "It's all down to this."

"What's 'this'?" Nicholas asked as he took the clipboard. He examined the paper.

"It's an insurance company requirement," Feingold said. "It states that you are aware 'the game' exists and that you are a willing participant in said game—so on and so forth."

"I'm a willing participant only if I decide to go ahead with this," Nicholas said.

"Of course," Feingold replied. "But we've never had anyone back out before. I don't imagine you'd want to be the first."

Nicholas ignored the bait. He'd been taunted by bigger and better. He skimmed the first paper and flipped to the second.

Feingold turned his head so he could read along with Nicholas. His face was close. There was pork lo mein on his breath.

"That's our guarantee," Feingold said. "It says that payment's entirely at your brother's discretion and that we understand it's a gift, with payment dependent upon your satisfaction."

"You mean, I don't like it, he doesn't pay."

"In essence, yes. But that's never happened," Feingold said quickly. "We've never had an unsatisfied customer."

"You mean *dis*satisfied," Nicholas said.

"That's right. You're a left-brain word fetishist."

"Am I?" Nicholas said. "Did the tests tell you that?"

Feingold smiled. He handed Nicholas the ballpoint pen. He flipped to the first page and pointed. "Initials here . . . here . . . and here. And . . . sign here."

Nicholas sighed and shook his head. "Sure. Why the hell not?"

He put the clipboard on the armrest of the chair. He was about to sign when Feingold suddenly grasped his wrist.

"In blood," Feingold said. "Like a deal with the devil." Then he smiled broadly. "Just kidding."

Nicholas shook his head and signed. When he was finished, Feingold tore out two pink-tinted pages and handed them to Nicholas.

"Your copies, thank you," he said. "Keep the pen as a memento." Feingold slipped the clipboard under his arm and offered Nicholas his hand. He shook it briefly and then backed quickly toward the door. "We'll let you know."

"Whatever," Nicholas said.

"The exit is right out this door to the left," Feingold said. "Thanks for coming," he said. Then he winked and was gone.

Nicholas shook his head again. "A grown man just winked at me," he muttered. He picked up his briefcase and, still not believing how he'd wasted his entire morning on this, he headed out the door and to the elevator.

chapter 9

Nicholas went to his office and worked through the afternoon. When evening arrived, he didn't feel like going right back home. He hadn't expended his full day's supply of energy. He could feel it in his chest, in his arms. He needed to let it out.

He went back to the squash club and played some woman he'd never seen before. She wasn't very good but she had a court and that was what mattered. He exhausted her after twenty-five minutes and then he had the court to himself. He ran through a series of drills for the next thirty-five minutes.

He was just out of a long, warm shower, standing by the mahogany locker, when his cellular phone rang. It was Conrad. He wanted to have dinner. This time, on him.

"What about Monday or Tuesday?" he asked.

"Bad for me," Nicholas said.

"How 'bout tonight?"

"I'll be working all evening. Got to make up for lost time. Next Wednesday's the only possibility right now."

"Okay," Conrad said. "Next Wednesday it is."

"I've got to make up time," Nicholas continued, "because I went to see your pals at C.R.S. today."

"Really? What did you think?"

"I think they're a bit disorganized and neurotic. The whole thing was pretty weird."

"I'm surprised. When I did it in London they'd been around for a while. Had everything down real pat."

"Not this group."

"You gonna do it?"

"I haven't decided yet," Nicholas said. "Look, I'm dripping all over the nice carpet here. I'll talk to you before Wednesday, okay?"

"Sure," Conrad said. "Bye."

Nicholas hung up. He put the phone back in his suit jacket and began toweling off. As he scrubbed at his scalp, two men arrived at the lockers behind him. They lay their racquets down and sat heavily as they pulled off their Nikes.

"It'd be a great opportunity to get in on the ground floor of what I think is going to be the next Disneyland," one of the men was saying.

"No argument, Gerard," said the other, "but C.R.S. will not go public. They're family-owned and plan to keep it that way."

"Stranger things have happened."

"No. They haven't, actually."

Nicholas stopped wiping his hair. He moved to his shoulders, eager to hear what they had to say.

"They've opened here, you know," said Gerard.

"The Game—in San Francisco?"

"Yup."

"You see?" said Ted, a bit sadly. "They're doing fine without any of us. The first toast tonight will be to them."

The men headed toward the showers. Nicholas turned slightly in order to catch sight of them before they disappeared. Both were tall with silver hair. He dressed quickly and headed to the dimly lit club lounge, where he presumed the men would be drinking. It was nearly empty, as it usually was around dinnertime.

The two men arrived fifteen minutes after Nicholas. He was nursing a Diet Coke at the bar; he rarely drank alcohol, and he never drank when he needed to be alert.

The men sat at one of the small tables in a corner. They ordered drinks from the waiter, carefully lit cigars with wooden matches from the table, and began talking loudly about the inadequacy of their squash and golf games.

Nicholas motioned over the bartender as he fixed their drinks.

"New members, Bobby?"

"I believe so, sir."

"Names?"

"I'm sorry, Mr. Van Orton," said the young bartender. "I only saw them once before."

"This round's on me," Nicholas said as he picked up his Diet Coke and walked to the table.

The men looked over as he approached. They put on small, pleasant smiles and took the cigars from their mouths. Midwesterners, Nicholas guessed from their fresh-scrubbed look and welcoming eyes.

"I hope I'm not intruding, gentlemen," Nicholas said when he was still several feet away. He didn't wait for an answer. Once he'd made up his mind about something, he never did. "I'm Nicholas Van Orton." He extended his hand.

"I'm Jerry Gill," Gerard said, accepting the hand, "and this is Ted Thurston."

Ted shook Nicholas's hand. "Care to pull up a seat?" he said.

Nicholas thanked him and borrowed a stool from the adjoining table. Definitely hick country, he decided: Gerard was polite and used the short, friendly versions of their names. Texas, he guessed, from the accent and the good, tall-in-the-saddle posture.

"I don't believe I've seen you here before," Nicholas said.

"We only joined last week," Ted replied. "Transferees from Dallas."

"Ah," Nicholas said. "You must be part of the Marius Group that just came out here."

"That's right," said Gerard. "You must be in finance or else you read the business pages pretty darn thoroughly."

"Both," said Nicholas.

"You need any stock advice?" Ted chuckled.

"That happens to be one thing I don't happen to need," Nicholas replied. "Now golf advice—that's another matter."

Gerard laughed as the drinks arrived. "Afraid you've come to the wrong place for that, Nick. Or is it Nicholas?"

"Nick is fine."

"Just wanted to make sure," Gerard said. "Some people don't like nicknames—no pun intended."

"Right," Nicholas smiled. Lord God, San Francisco was going to eat these rubes alive.

"No," Gerard said as he rolled his cigar between his lips. "I definitely can't help you with your swing. The last time I played Pebble I swore I'd never pick up a club again."

"Golf isn't my game either," Ted added.

"Speaking of games," Nicholas said, hunching closer, "I couldn't help but overhear you talking about C.R.S. in the locker room."

The pair's pleasant demeanor vanished suddenly, the eyes losing their sparkle and their big smiles drooping a bit. They exchanged a furtive glance and put their cigars back in their mouths.

"Just a bit of chinwag," said Gerard.

"Sure, sure," Nicholas said. *Chinwag*, he thought. *Jesus H.* "I only mention it because I happened to take their tests this morning, at the office on Montgomery Street."

The men suddenly looked interested.

"Did you?" asked Ted. "Kudos."

"Your Game hasn't started yet?" Gerard asked.

"No, it hasn't," Nicholas said.

Ted glanced down and then away. After a moment he

looked behind him as if he were simply taking in the room. Then he looked down again. The whole thing struck Nicholas as what you did when you wanted to check out someone behind you without seeming to. Bad P.I. stuff.

Nicholas moved in closer. The men also leaned forward. He suddenly felt conspiratorial. "I was actually kind of hoping that you two could tell me . . . exactly what is the Game?"

"Ahhh," said Gerard. "What is it?"

"The eternal question," said Ted.

"I envy you," said Gerard.

Ted raised his glass. "Ditto."

Tweedledee and Tweedledum came to mind. *Alice* seemed to be the motif of the day.

"I tell you, gentlemen, I wish I could go back and do it for the first time all over again," Gerard said. He raised his own glass. "Here's to—C.R.S., because we promised."

Gerard and Ted both took sips.

"And here's to new experiences," Ted said.

The men raised their glasses again and drained them in a single gulp. Gerard brought his glass down in front of him. Then he placed both hands flat on the table and rose slowly.

"Man," he said, "I'm gonna be sore tomorrow. These balls don't bounce the way racquetballs do." He looked at Nicholas. "If you'll excuse me, I've got to be going. I have to prepare for a very early breakfast meeting." He offered his hand to Nicholas. "Good night, Nick. Nice meeting you."

"The same," Nicholas said, shaking his hand.

Gerard wished Ted a good night, promised to beat his ass next time, then scooped up his gym bag and left. Ted sat up straight again and turned his attention to his cigar.

Nicholas regarded him through the smoke. "Tell me," Nicholas said, "did you play recently?"

Ted puffed then nodded. "It was about a year ago. I was working in Los Angeles."

"Los Angeles? How many branches do these people have?"

Ted shook his head and shrugged. "Private company. Extremely private. No one knows for sure."

"I've heard good things about their London branch." He sipped his Diet Coke. "You have to admit, it sounds like some fantasy, role-playing nonsense."

Ted snickered. He leaned in again. "You want to know what it is? What it's all about?"

"Yes, I do."

"I'll tell you," he said. He enjoyed his cigar for a moment and then said, "John. Chapter nine. Verse twenty-five."

"Sorry, Ted," Nicholas said. "I haven't been to Sunday school in years."

Ted grinned. " 'Whereas once I was blind, now I can see.' " He rose and picked up his gym bag. "I've got to be at that same breakfast meeting."

He reached for his wallet but Nicholas held up his hand.

"Thanks, Nick," Ted said graciously. "Next time's on me. Best of luck, y'hear?"

"Thanks," Nicholas said as Ted left the lounge.

Nicholas sat alone in the now-empty lounge. Alone with his Diet Coke, his scattered thoughts, and the curious words from John.

The setting sun gleamed outside the large conference room window on the top floor of the Van Orton Group Building. Nicholas sat at one end of the thick, smoked glass table that nearly filled the room. Behind him stood the silver-haired Mr. Sutherland, his tall, lean imperturbable attorney. Three other very young, very dapper lawyers sat on either side of the table.

A thick contract sat on the table in front of Nicholas. He used a red felt-tipped pen to amend it. Ruthlessly.

"If the Baer/Grant meeting does not take place tomorrow," Nicholas said as he wrote, "it might as well never take place at all. Please make sure that your client and his principal stockholders are aware of that fact."

"They understand," said one of the attorneys.

Nicholas put his pen down, closed the document, and slid it to the lawyer nearest him on his right. "There you are, Mr. Grantham. Now your document is acceptable to the Van Orton Group."

The other attorneys got up and gathered behind Bill Grantham.

"When Mr. Van Orton boards his plane tomorrow," Sutherland said, "every agreement and addendum will be typed into your document. The complete closing package, flawlessly revised." He leaned close to Nicholas. "This is why we're paid twice what we deserve. So that you will miss another opera you'd have fallen asleep during anyway."

"I happen to like opera," Nicholas replied. "It's just too bad they're doing *Die Meistersinger von Nurnberg* tonight. They're starting early because it runs over five-and-a-half hours."

"In that case, my apologies," Sutherland said. "Look at this, then, as an opportunity to show our client how well we will rise to his exhilarating challenge of providing an inadequate document at the last minute."

"We just won't tell them that we work better under pressure," Nicholas said as his cellular phone rang. He frowned as he fished it out of his inside jacket pocket. "Yes?"

"Nicholas Van Orton?" the caller asked.

"Yes. Who is this?"

"This is Cynthia calling from C.R.S."

It took a moment to place the name. He hadn't thought about C.R.S. all day. "How did you get this number?" he asked.

She ignored the question. "We've finished processing your application, Mr. Van Orton—"

"I'm in a meeting!" he snapped.

"I'm afraid it was rejected," she continued.

Nicholas was silent for a moment. "Pardon me?"

"You shouldn't feel this reflects negatively on you," she said. "We hope we haven't caused you any inconvenience."

"Inconvenience? This is absurd!"

"I'm sorry," she said insincerely. "Thank you for thinking of C.R.S."

The woman hung up. Nicholas folded the phone and put it back in his pocket. *Rejected? Who the hell were these sons of bitches?*

"Anything wrong?" Sutherland asked.

"No. Nothing at all. I'm fine."

Nicholas was lying and he knew it, though he didn't understand *why* he was upset. A group of looney tunes had decided that he was unfit for something. That was hardly a snub.

So why did it feel like one?

After the meeting Nicholas canceled dinner with Sutherland. He called Ilsa and told her to make dinner, the usual, then headed to his car. Before he pulled out, he called the Sheraton Palace Hotel and asked for Conrad. He was out and his room voice mail answered.

"Hi, this is Conrad. Please leave a message after the tone. Thanks. Bye."

"Connie, it's Nicholas," he said after the beep. "Give me a ring when you can." He hesitated, trying to decide whether to tell him the truth or whether to spin it. "About your birthday gift," he said. "Things are really crazy right now. I'm not sure it'll fit my schedule. Anyway, I'll see you at dinner tomorrow, same place, same table." Guiltily, for having lied, he added, "Looking forward to it."

He hung up.

Twilight turned to darkness. The drive home was filled with quiet Chopin preludes and harshly muttered words about "chicken-shit" Feingold, the "high-fat Chinese food he stuffed into his fat head," and his "seriously fucked staff of morons." Nicholas was still pissed off as he neared his driveway and pressed the button to open the gate.

The gate moved slowly inward. As soon as it had opened sufficiently, Nicholas steered the BMW impatiently around it. And stopped suddenly.

Just outside the reach of the headlight beams, to the right, he saw a dark shape on the lawn. Nicholas jumped when he realized that it looked like a body clothed in a dark overcoat—or a robe. He had visions of his father lying facedown in nearly the same place almost forty years before.

His heart slamming against his throat, Nicholas got out of the car. The thing on the lawn was definitely a body, though it wasn't moving. As an afterthought, he went back into the car and got his squash racquet from the gym bag. He clutched it tightly as he approached.

"Hello!" Nicholas said. "What are you doing there? How'd you get in?"

It still didn't move. Nicholas clapped his hands hard. Still nothing.

"Wonderful," he said. Taking a deep breath, he crossed the driveway to the edge of the lawn.

The spotlights were turned on outside the kitchen but they didn't reach to the front of the mansion. Nicholas approached warily. He wondered why Ilsa hadn't heard his shouts.

She's getting old, he thought. Not like Nicholas. He was getting younger. He felt as if he were ten years old again, walking toward his father's body to see if he'd survived. *Of course he survived,* Nicholas remembered thinking. This was Dad. Nothing ever happened to dads. Nothing.

But the elder Van Orton hadn't survived. And part of Nicholas had died that day too. The part that believed anything could be secure.

The back of the body was facing him. Nicholas was now just a few feet away from it. He saw now that the figure was definitely wearing a robe. A robe just like the one his father had been wearing.

"Are you okay?" Nicholas said. "Because if you are, I'm gonna split your goddamned skull for fucking around here."

There was no response. Nicholas stopped directly behind the body and nudged it tentatively with his toe. It didn't respond. He crouched slowly. Holding the squash racquet above his head, he reached out and gently lay a hand upon the body's shoulder. He shook it, half-expecting whoever it was to turn and gasp or scream. It didn't move. His breath shallow and his heart still racing, Nicholas grasped the coat and pulled it toward him.

The figure flopped over lightly. Nicholas leapt back with alarm which quickly became anger as he regarded the face.

The body was a wooden mannequin, its face painted to resemble the clown who had made the balloon animals at Nicholas's seventh birthday party. Nicholas rose. With a sneer, he reached down, grabbed the figure by the front of its robe, and lifted it off the lawn.

He trudged toward the house wondering who could have done this and why. Conrad? Not even at his druggiest would he have made a joke of their father's memory. Elizabeth? Ilsa? Maria?

Oh come on*, man.*

But the clown mannequin *was* here and someone had put it there. He wondered if he should have left it where it was and called his friend Detective Gorbaty at the SFPD.

He went in the front entrance, disengaged the alarm, and dumped the mannequin on a bench just inside the doorway. He turned on the light. As he did he noticed something sticking from the mannequin's mouth. A red ribbon of some kind. He put his keys back in his pocket and went over to the clown.

Bending over the face, he studied the ribbon. Only an inch was sticking from a narrow slit in the hinged mouth. He wondered what would happen if he pulled it. The damn thing might explode.

No, he decided. If someone wanted to kill him, they wouldn't have bothered with the doll. They could have rigged the door or his car or his dinner.

"The old bomb-in-a-cheeseburger bit," he snickered as he pulled on the ribbon. It came out slowly: there was something heavy on the other end. He continued to tug on it. Finally, a key slid out—gold, not brass. And embossed on the top were three letters:

    C.R.S.

Nicholas sat in his chair with his dinner tray at his side and the television turned to CNN. The key sat on the table beside the remote controls. Every now and then he'd pick it up and just stare at it.

The light hadn't been on in the guest house. Once in a while Ilsa went out with a "gentleman caller," and he assumed that was where she was. He also assumed that the mannequin had been deposited in her absence. C.R.S. guys must have been watching the house.

So why did they tell him he'd failed the tests?

He didn't know. He watched the TV, his mind wandering.

"The President warned today that passage of this legislation will affect millions of Americans," the anchorman was saying, "with a resulting rise in unemployment and decline in viable small businesses. Meanwhile, Republican leaders argued that its passage would be the very stimulant a sluggish economy needs. No one has expressed an opinion as to how it will impact the pampered existence of Nicholas Van Orton."

Nicholas squinted over at the TV. The anchorman had moved on to a story about the price of tea in China. He couldn't have heard what he thought he had heard. He was just tired and distracted.

And angry.

Chomping down on the last remaining french fries, he looked over at the clown on the bench in the adjoining hallway. Then he picked up the knife from his tray and walked over. He sat the figure up so that the light shined directly on the face. Then he pulled down the lower jaw and stuck the blade into the opening. He slid it back and forth and back as far as it would go.

"The one thing on which both Democrats and Republicans seem to agree," the anchorman continued, "is that most Americans harbor serious doubts about the economic future. A recent poll suggests a staggering fifty-seven percent of American workers believe there is a very real chance they will be unemployed within the next five-to-seven years. But what does that matter to a bloated, millionaire fat cat like you?"

Nicholas looked up. He heard that. He hurried back to the library. The anchorman was reporting as usual, nothing strange. Nicholas looked at the TV for a moment more.

"Right," he said. "The anchorman's talking about you, Nick. Baer/Grant is big international damn news." Shaking his head, he started walking slowly back toward the hallway.

"In other financial news," the anchorman said, "stock markets rose both domestically and abroad today after the announcement of stronger-than-expected earnings by several high-tech companies, but then dipped down, reacting to reports that Nicholas Van Orton was in a bad mood."

Nicholas spun, disbelieving. "What the fuck—?"

The anchorman looked over at him. "Are you going to spend the rest of the evening prying at that clown's mouth?"

Nicholas's own mouth felt unhinged. "I— I don't . . ."

"You don't *what*?" he demanded. "You don't believe this?

Well, I have to tell you. It's very frustrating for me if you don't even pretend to pay attention."

Nicholas held the knife tightly in his right hand as he marched toward the television. "What is this?"

The anchorman smiled coolly. "This is your Game, Nicholas, and welcome to it. I'm here to let you in on a few ground rules."

As Nicholas neared the TV screen, he noticed ripples and artifacts in the image. He knelt in front of it, his hands on either side. The face was computer-generated. A fake. But someone was tuned into the room somehow, watching and listening. He stood and looked around.

"Rather than try and figure *me* out," the anchorman went on, "why don't we move on to what really matters?"

"Fair enough," Nicholas said angrily. "Why don't you tell me what really matters?"

"You received the first key. Others will follow. You never know where you'll find them or when or how you'll need to use them, so keep your eyes open."

"Eyes open," Nicholas repeated. He was getting really sore. His privacy had been invaded and he wanted to know how. "Look, fella. Before I buy any of what you're saying, I want to know how you see and hear me."

"I see you, I hear you," he said. "That's all that matters."

"Not to me."

"Why don't we save the questions till—"

"No, now. How does this work?"

The anchorman smiled. "All right. There's a tiny camera looking at you right now."

"That's impossible. You couldn't have gotten in here. The security system is on all day, even when Ilsa is here."

"You're right," the anchorman agreed. "It's impossible. You're having a conversation with your television, just like you do every night."

Nicholas walked back over. He felt around the sides of the picture tube, then examined the cable box.

"The camera is miniaturized," the anchorman said. "Fiber optics with a pretty darn small lens."

Nicholas looked closely at the side-mounted stereo speakers. He began prying the plastic face from one.

"Do you know how dangerous that is?" the anchorman asked.

"No. Tell me!" Nicholas barked.

"Tell you what?" a voice asked from behind.

Nicholas rose and spun. Ilsa was standing in the doorway. She was dressed in a dark sweatshirt, jeans, and athletic shoes. Her white hair was pulled into a slightly mussed bun.

"Yes," she said. "I was taking a bath and I thought I heard you yelling."

"In domestic news," said the anchorman, "Detroit auto workers vowed to remain on picket lines after day ten of what looks to be a lengthy strike. . . ."

Ilsa took a few small steps into the library. She looked down at the knife. "Is everything all right, Mr. Van Orton?"

"Oh, sure," he said. "Fine."

"In Southern California," the anchorman said, "firefighters are struggling to bring under control a major fire that broke out in a petroleum processing plant yesterday. Several workers were injured in the explosion that started the blaze. . . ."

"Your dinner was all right?" Ilsa asked.

"Of course. As always."

She nodded suspiciously. "Then unless you need anything else, I'll be leaving for the evening."

"I'm all set," Nicholas said, "thank you. And good night."

"Good night, then," Ilsa said.

She turned and left.

"A commuter plane which crashed overnight in North Carolina came within one hundred yards of a suburban apartment building," the anchorman said. "Heavy weather is said to be the cause. . . ."

The kitchen slider opened. It shut heavily.

The anchorman stopped reading the news. He looked up at Nicholas. "Who was that?"

"Never mind who that was."

"You're uncomfortable."

"You're perceptive."

"You really want to know how a camera got into your home, don't you?" the anchorman asked.

"Yes. Yes, I do."

The anchorman smiled and then vanished suddenly. In his place was a fish-eye view of the room. It was not from the TV's point-of-view: the camera was somewhere to the right, near the entrance.

Nicholas crossed the room toward the bookcases. He kept his eye on the TV, using it as a guide.

"Cold, cold . . . ," came the anchorman's voice.

Nicholas stopped. He moved toward the doorway.

"Warmer, warmer . . . ," said the voice.

Nicholas looked around. He was near the hallway. He looked back at the TV. He could see his entire body sideways. He sidled toward the doorway. He grew larger, the top of his head disappearing off the screen. He continued moving in that direction. His head vanished entirely.

He turned toward the hallway. And looked right into the dead eyes of the clown.

With an oath, Nicholas dove over with the knife. Grabbing the back of the figure's head, he scooped out the left eye. It popped free easily, clattered to the floor, and rolled toward the door. He pried out the right eye. Something prevented it from coming free. Nicholas looked behind it and saw a wire about the thickness and consistency of dental floss. He plucked it out and threw the mannequin back against the bench.

"This brings us to the end of our broadcasting day," he sneered as the crackle of static came from the library. Feeling a sense of triumph, of being back in control of things, Nicholas turned and walked back toward the TV. But the sense of wellness evaporated as he looked at the glittering picture tube.

The snow and static vanished. The picture turned a solid blue. A telephone number appeared on the screen.

The old *Outer Limits* TV show came to mind as Nicholas realized that even the static had been under the control of C.R.S. *Do not attempt to adjust the picture. . . .*

The anchorman's voice returned. "Write this number down," it suggested. The voice was more insistent now than playful or sarcastic. "It's a twenty-four-hour Consumer Recreation Services hot line, for emergencies only. But don't call asking what the object of the Game is. Figuring that out is the object of the Game."

Nicholas walked over to a sofa in the middle of the room. He made a conscious effort to *walk,* not run. Even though the bastards couldn't see him anymore, he didn't want to give in to even a hint of panic. His jacket was draped over the armrest. He picked it up and reached into his pocket. He withdrew a valet parking stub and the C.R.S. ballpoint pen. He dutifully recorded the number and then slipped the stub into his pants pocket.

"Good luck and congratulations on choosing C.R.S.," the anchorman's voice said. "We now return you to your regularly scheduled program."

The blue screen and the number winked off. They were replaced by the real CNN anchorman.

". . . threatened to have the American ambassador expelled after the incident. The U.S. State Department responded quickly with a formal apology and an announcement of the ambassador's immediate removal. No word yet on the chosen replacement. In France, the driest conditions in over forty years have taken a toll on the country's agricultural heartland. . . ."

But Nicholas didn't hear any of it. He was looking down at the telephone number. Whether he wanted it or not, he was in the Game.

It was the first time Nicholas had ever been on the roof. As a young child he'd never been permitted there. After his father's death it was years before he could even look up at it.

The roof was not a place Nicholas had ever expected to find himself. But the first thing he'd had to decide this evening was whether or not to conform to the pattern he followed every night. Whether that would be helping or hindering his opponents—for that was how he now viewed them. Nicholas had decided to take the offensive, which meant not following his routine. And that was how he'd ended up on the roof. He'd already seen some of C.R.S.'s technological capabilities. Finding the uplink the company had used to gain control of his TV might tell him more about them.

The answer was disappointingly simple. With a large flashlight under his arm, he crawled over to the satellite dish near the chimney. Tucked against the base of the dish he found a box with a rabbit ear antenna. That was the receiver, from wherever they were broadcasting. Probably the place on Montgomery. It was attached to the output jack by a short length of coaxial cable.

All it took was to screw it in. Nothing fancy.

Nicholas reached down and began to unscrew it, then stopped. What if they needed to contact him again? He decided to leave it alone. Besides, they were probably watching him—from the street, from a tree, from behind the guest house; maybe in person, maybe with another camera.

He backed along the sloping roof toward the ladder. He carefully placed his foot on the rung second from the top; it would be pretty pathetic, he thought, if the Game ended with him falling from the roof just minutes after it had begun. Conrad would never let him forget it.

Nicholas lay the ladder down on the ground and went to the mansion's back door. Once through it, he shut it, locked it, and punched the alarm code in the keypad. Then he went upstairs to bed.

Nicholas slept well.

The following morning he woke early and headed south on 101 to San Francisco International Airport. Sutherland would be meeting him at the gate with the updated contract.

"Help me out there?" a homeless man said as Nicholas reached the terminal. "I used to be an affluent fella till some folks did this to me—"

Nicholas noticed him but walked past him.

"Yeah, Mr. Moneybags, ignore me like everybody else."

Nicholas continued to ignore him. He walked purposefully through the automatic door to the busy terminal. He felt as if he were noticing everyone this morning. A man and a woman talking in sign language. A man staring into space behind an open newspaper. A janitor with a big, rattling key chain. A man at a pay phone who Nicholas could have sworn was staring at him.

I've got it, he thought. *The Game is pure paranoia. They*

*don't do a thing after the initial visit from the anchorman.
They just make you think they're going to do something.*

Nicholas reached the security checkpoint. He lay his briefcase on the conveyor belt of the X-ray machine and put his keys, cellular phone, and Patek Phillipe watch in the tray. He passed through the metal detector and the security guard brought the tray to him.

"Nice watch," the man said.

Nicholas smiled tolerantly as he collected his belongings. He looked back at the belt. As he watched, it stopped. His briefcase was on the monitor.

"Is there a problem?" Nicholas asked the female guard.

She looked back at him, expressionless. She turned the belt back on. His briefcase spilled down the ramp and he picked it up. He looked at his watch, saw that he had time, and headed to the Golden Air lounge.

The lounge was dark, with red carpets and thick-cushioned white chairs. He took a complimentary cup of coffee, black, and sat beside a coffee table. Two seats away a middle-aged man in a smartly tailored suit coughed, then rose as Nicholas sat. From the corner of his eye, Nicholas saw the man drop his newspaper on the empty seat between them. Nicholas glanced over as the man left. His brow knit as he noticed an infant's rattle beneath the newspaper: painted on the side was a smiling clown face.

Nicholas looked up. He only caught a glimpse of the man from behind as he exited the lounge. He was a tall man with silver hair—just like the Texans from the squash club lounge, now that he thought of it.

Just like a lot of men, Nicholas told himself, annoyed with his creeping paranoia.

He picked up the rattle and studied it, looking for another key. He shook it at arm's length, then a little closer, then held it up to the light of the central chandelier to try and see through it.

"Excuse me," a bell-delicate voice said from beside him.

71

He looked up and saw a young woman with a baby in her arms.

"That's mine," she said. "Actually, his." She pointed to the rattle and then to the baby.

"Oh, I'm so very sorry," Nicholas said, embarrassed.

He handed the rattle to the woman then put his forehead in his palms and pressed. He listened to the *chuck, chuck, chuck* of the rattle as she crossed the lounge. When she was gone, he looked up. His eyes settled on a bespectacled man who was watching him from across the coffee table.

Watching him or merely observing some pretty odd proceedings?

Nicholas turned away. He had to stop this now. Taking the "offensive" wasn't going to work. He was going to have to let the Game—whatever this "Game" was—come to him, not anticipate it.

He took a swallow of coffee and set it down. He noticed the bespectacled man still looking at him. Not observing but definitely staring.

Nicholas leaned across the table. "May I *help* you?" he snapped.

His tone caused other heads to turn. The bespectacled man looked around, adjusted his glasses nervously, then tapped his own chest.

"What!" Nicholas yelled. "What is it?"

The man tapped his chest again. Then he pointed to Nicholas.

Nicholas looked down. A big blue ink stain had formed on the inside of his jacket. The ink had seeped through the fabric of his pocket, causing a big blue splotch on his white shirt. Swearing, he reached inside his suit and removed the leaking pen. It was the ballpoint pen he'd picked up at C.R.S. Swearing again, he dropped the pen in his coffee cup, snatched up his briefcase, and left the lounge.

The men's room was right next door and Nicholas tried in vain to scrub the stain using wet paper towels. All he managed to do was smear it around until the shirt was more blue than white. He was going to have to see if there was a men's shop somewhere in the terminal.

Disgusted, he picked up his briefcase and turned to go.

"Hey, buddy—you still out there?"

Nicholas stopped and looked around. He was alone except for a man in one of the stalls. All he could see was the man's brown shoes. Common sense told Nicholas to leave. But common sense was not in control at the moment.

"I'm in a little bit of trouble," the man continued. "Could you c'mere?" A large hairy hand dropped down below the stall door, motioning him over. "I ain't no perv, mister, I just need paper. There's none in here."

Nicholas hurried from the rest room. And ran smack into Sutherland.

"There you are!" said the attorney. "I was beginning to worry." His eyes lowered. "Trying to set a new fashion trend, Nicholas?"

"Very funny," Nicholas said. "You happen to see a men's shop anywhere around here?"

"Afraid not. Ask the driver when you land. I'm sure he can help. With any luck you'll be the same size."

"Even funnier," Nicholas said.

Sutherland handed him the thick contract.

"Up all night on this?" Nicholas asked.

"A goodly portion thereof," the attorney admitted. "I checked it personally. It's a masterpiece of legalese."

"I'm sure it is," Nicholas said, bending and slipping it into his briefcase. "Now go home and get some sleep."

"You're certain you don't want me along? Seattle can be such an unforgiving place."

"Please," Nicholas said. "I'll be fine."

The men shook hands and Sutherland turned to go. Nicholas checked the monitor for his gate and hurried over.

He was guessing that the stares now were due to his shirt.

At least that's what he told himself as he boarded the plane, settled into seat 1A, threw a blanket over his benighted chest, and closed his eyes—more to shut the world out than to shut himself in.

chapter 13

H e looked like a penguin with few and plastered hairs. Anson Baer was round-bellied and pale-cheeked, the bald center of his head covered with ivory-white strands of hair combed to the right. He was dressed in a three-piece suit with a watch chain and suede shoes. The only color was a lopsided red bow tie.

He was glaring at Nicholas from across his large, ornately carved desk. Wearing a new white shirt, his jacket buttoned, Nicholas was pacing slowly beside standees of Baer/Grant's popular children's book characters, from the ice-cream-loving monster, God'nilla, to the basketball-playing bears, the NetFurs. There were also a series of educational titles, *Math Marvels* and *Word Wonders*, stacked in Little Baer Books counter displays.

"All these years," Baer said through his laminated teeth, "and the first time ever you step foot in these offices it's to ask me to step down?"

Nicholas shrugged. "You promised you'd meet projections, Anson. A dollar-sixty per share, you said. I don't think this is so surprising a visit."

"Projections were far too optimistic," Baer replied hotly.

"Admittedly—"

"Our EPS was one-fifty last quarter. We're up eight cents a share."

"But the expectation was ten," Nicholas pointed out. "And in this case, Mr. Baer, expectation is everything."

"Now it's 'Mr.,'" Baer said. "Fine, *Mr.* Van Orton. Will you really hold me to it over pennies?"

"My stock in Baer/Grant is falling. Isn't yours? Those pennies are costing me millions."

"Only for now," Baer said. "You know damn well the stock will turn."

"It probably will," Nicholas admitted. "In fact, I'd say it almost certainly will—in time."

"Then give me until next quarter," Baer said, softening. "If you still feel this way, vote your shares."

"Mr. Baer—Anson—unfortunately, today is what counts."

Baer slapped his desk. "You snot-nosed son of a bitch! If your father could see you now."

Nicholas stopped pacing. "What?"

"Your father was a good, close friend," Baer went on. "Goddamn it—I watched you grow up. I came to your birthday parties! How do you end up treating me like this?"

Nicholas's mouth tightened. "Did you think that what we have between us is friendship?"

"I made that mistake, yes."

"Why? Because you came to my birthdays and went fishing with my father? Is that any reason why I should sit on my hands while you throw my money away? Not just my money, but the money of dozens of shareholders?"

"Now, look—"

"I'm not through, but I will be in a minute. You misspoke before, Mr. Baer. You're not 'stepping down.' The whole point of my visit is to demonstrate that you're not deciding anything anymore. I'm firing you. Action is taken. Confidence is restored. Stock goes up. The fact that you're an old 'family friend' makes my point even more sharply."

"Judas Nicholas Iscariot—"

"Yeah, well, that's life."

"There is no Baer/Grant Publishing without Anson Baer."

"You think not? Where's Stewart Grant? He's gone sailing. He's out there enjoying his golden years probably wondering where the hell you are." Nicholas picked up his briefcase from between Steve Grizzly and Polar Laurie of the NetFurs. He pushed some papers aside on the desk and lay the briefcase there. He tried popping it open. "You're about to join him, old friend. Because you've failed. The severance I'm offering is more than equitable." He struggled with the latch as he spoke. "Dig up a notary and sign. The offer's valid for tonight only."

"I could fight you on this," Baer said.

"You sure could. But if I leave without your signature, this agreement—if I can get it the fuck out—begins to disintegrate. Benefits shrink, options narrow, compensation shrivels." He stood the briefcase on end and slammed his right palm-heel down against the latches. They refused to open. "This is in your best interest," he said, hitting the latches again. Still nothing. It occurred to him then that the briefcase might be locked, though he couldn't remember having done that. He removed his key case and unsnapped it. He was surprised to find the C.R.S. key on the hook where he kept the briefcase key. He didn't remember having put it there. Perhaps he had; the previous night had been pretty disorienting. The key didn't look like it would fit but he tried it anyway. He got the tip in and tried to turn it. Nothing happened.

Baer smirked cruelly. "I hope, young Van Orton, you plan on running the company better than that."

"Your problem, Mr. Baer, is that you can't tell the difference between a glitch and a management style," he said angrily, hurtfully. He glared at the older man. "As luck would have it you've gotten a temporary stay of execution.

77

But that's all it is, 'old friend.' I'll get a copy to you via overnight. I've accomplished what I came here for."

"Did you come here to prove yourself a heartless little prick?" Baer asked coldly.

"Good morning, sir," Nicholas said, pulling his briefcase from the desk and knocking over a bookended row of thin Little Baer volumes.

Nicholas left the office, left the suite, left the building in a quick and furious blur. Upon reaching the street, he stopped. He wanted that goddamn old fart's signature on the contract. *That* was why he'd come, dammit! Except for this fucking stupid briefcase he'd *have* it.

In a rage, he raised the briefcase above his head and smashed it down hard on a fire hydrant.

The briefcase thunked loudly but didn't dent. Grunting with anger and ignoring the pedestrians who were walking in a wide arc around him, Nicholas stalked over to the waiting limousine and ordered the driver to get him the hell out of Seattle.

Nicholas sat at the table, his near-empty Diet Coke in front of him. He poked absently at the lemon with his straw. Then he checked his watch.

It was 7:55. Conrad was nearly a half hour late. That was typical of the old Conrad, who usually got held up because of some drug deal or else was too drugged out even to *get* up. Nicholas had thought the new Conrad would be different. He didn't know who he was more disappointed in: Conrad or himself for believing that his brother might have changed.

No one changes, he thought as he drained his glass.

He raised his hand and motioned over the portly, mustachioed maître d'. "Is there a message up front from my brother Conrad?"

"Not that I'm aware of, Mr. Van Orton. But I'll check."

Nicholas looked out the window. His battered briefcase was beside him on the seat. He couldn't wait to get home and pry the thing open. Destroy it. Punish it for having tormented him.

"To hell with Conrad," he decided suddenly. He grabbed the briefcase handle and slid from the booth.

And collided with a waitress who was carrying a tray of red wine. The two glasses fell over, pouring wine onto Nicholas's jacket.

"Oh, excuse me!" the waitress gasped. She set the tray on the table and reached for a napkin. "I'm so, so sorry, sir." She placed a hand on the inside of his jacket and began blotting the outside.

"Please don't do that," Nicholas said testily. He pulled away.

"It'll just take a sec—"

"I said *don't*!" He snatched the napkin away from her. "I'll take care of this myself!"

"I do apologize, sir," she said. "I'm really having a bad day."

"A bad week," Nicholas replied. "You did the exact same thing to me the other day"—he glanced at her name tag—"Christine."

The young woman looked at him. She took a step back and swallowed. "Oh my God. I'm sorry."

"Save it. All I want from you are more napkins and some soda water."

"All right. Again, I'm sorry. It was an accident."

"Yeah. Terrific."

She regarded him a moment longer. "Look, I said I was sorry. It's not the end of the damn world."

"This jacket cost more than you make in a month," he replied, turning his back on her. "Don't tell me what's the end of the world or not."

"Fine! I won't!" she said, turning her own back and adding, "Asshole."

Nicholas spun. He stepped after her. "What did you say?"

"Are you deaf as well as rude?" she said. "I called you an asshole! Make that frigging asshole."

The maître d' arrived, his eyes wide. "Christine!" he shouted. "How *dare* you! Mr. Van Orton is a valued customer!"

"Then you kiss his ass," she said as she breezed past him.

The maître d' grabbed her arm above the elbow. "Don't talk to me like that, young woman!"

Christine fixed her eyes on the rotund man. "I apologized to him," she replied quietly, evenly. I offered to help. 'Mr.' Van Orton spoke abusively to me. He deserved what he got."

The maître d' stiffened. "And so shall you. Clean out your locker. At once, Miss Whitlock!"

Christine wrenched her arm away. "Fine, Dennis. Just as soon as I get my money for this week."

"Wait in my office," he said curtly. "I'll be right with you."

"I'll be counting the seconds, Mr. Mikasa," she said as she disappeared through the door.

The maître d' motioned over a pair of busboys, then smoothly guided Nicholas to a new table. "I'm terribly sorry, Mr. Van Orton," he said. "If you're not too uncomfortable, will this table suit you for a complimentary meal?"

"Yes," Nicholas said. "Fine." He was exhausted. And hungry. He was willing to do anything to end this maddening scene, this insane day.

"I'll fetch you a new waiter," he said.

"Also more napkins and soda water," Nicholas said.

"At once," the maître d' said.

Nicholas removed his jacket and draped it across the back of the chair. He slid into the seat and dug his palms into his eyes. He was hoping now that Conrad didn't show. All he wanted to do was eat, go home, and go to sleep. Even his goddamn briefcase could wait. He'd let Sutherland take care of getting a copy of the contract to Baer.

A waiter approached the table with a menu under his arm. Nicholas sat up. The waiter stopped and placed a check on the table. Then he walked away.

Nicholas stared after him. "Wait! Excuse me!"

The waiter didn't stop.

"Oh, *man!*" Nicholas threw up a hand. He looked down at the check. A message was scrawled in pencil across the front: *DON'T LET HER GET AWAY.* Nicholas looked up as the waiter went down the stairs beneath an *Exit* sign. "Hey! Waiter! *Wait!*"

But the young man was gone. Rising, Nicholas grabbed his briefcase and hurried through the restaurant. He heard a door close loudly. He reached the stairs and took them quickly. When he reached the door, he opened it and stepped outside into a dark alley. The door slammed shut behind him.

Nicholas looked around. The street was to the right. A high brick wall was to the left. Between himself and the street was another door. He began walking toward it. As he did, it opened and Christine stepped out.

"Yeah? Well fuck you and your vichyssoise, prick!" the young woman yelled. She kicked the door shut then glowered at it. "Goddamn maître d'ass-pain. I hope you choke on a chicken bone." She threw her bag over her shoulder and started toward the street.

Nicholas walked after her. "Pardon me—miss?"

She turned without stopping. "Oh, no. *You!*" She picked up the pace.

"Please wait!" Nicholas cried. He started after her, still holding the check the waiter had given him. "I got a note—I'm not sure how this works. Do you have something for me?"

"Sure, psycho. It's here between fingers two and four." She held up her hand as she kept walking.

"No, I mean—I want to know what's going on. Are you part of this?"

"What the hell are you talking about?" she asked. "Thanks to you, you know what I'm part of? Unemployment."

"I'm sorry about that," he said, still following her, "but I need to explain."

"Don't explain anything," she said as they neared the street. "Just fuck off. Now good-bye."

Nicholas reached for her and stepped into a deep, water-filled pothole. He stumbled, dropping his briefcase, hurting his knee, and drenching his pant leg. By the time he got up, the woman was rounding the corner of the alley.

"Goddammit!" he shouted. "I was trying to apologize! Can't you at least let me do that?"

She continued down the street. She did not look back.

Nicholas hung his head down. His shoulders sagged. "Jesus Christ," he said. He picked up his briefcase and turned slowly, heading back the way he'd come. He hadn't taken more than a few steps when he heard a strangled cry from the street. It was a man's voice. Nicholas turned in time to see a heavyset man drop to his knees beneath a streetlight and then fall forward on his face.

Nicholas instinctively began moving toward him. It looked as if the fellow had had a heart attack. Nicholas pulled his cellular phone from his pocket. It was damp from the wine. He hoped it still worked. As he flipped it open, the waitress returned. She bent beside the man.

"Christine!" Nicholas said. "Do you know this man?"

She shook her head. "What's with him?"

"I don't know. He just cried out and he fell."

The young woman knelt and tried to turn him on his side. Nicholas helped her and she was able to get an arm out from under him. She felt for a pulse.

Suddenly, the man began to convulse. Christine and Nicholas both jumped back.

"Do you have any idea what to do?" she asked.

The man fell silent. He didn't move.

"I think he's stopped breathing," Nicholas said.

Christine was already moving as he spoke. She stuck two fingers in his mouth and, grunting, dug them down his throat. She pulled thick saliva and mucous from his airway.

Nicholas handed her his handkerchief. She snatched it. "What the hell are you waiting for?" she asked.

"What?"

"Use the goddamn phone to dial 911!"

Nicholas had forgotten about the cellular. He picked it up and punched in the numbers. "This can't be real," he said, rising.

"The guy's pissing his pants. Is that real enough for you?"

"All right," Nicholas said. "Okay."

"And now he's fucking turning *blue*! Shit!"

Christine bent again and flopped the man onto his back. As she began giving him CPR, Nicholas found himself starting to believe. This wasn't a game. This was real.

"Damn!" he said as static filled the earpiece. What the hell good were these things if you couldn't use them in the heart of one of the busiest cities in the world? He started walking and then jogging down the street, attempting to catch a line. He stepped off the sidewalk but jumped back to the curb as a van barely missed him, its horn blaring.

"Freakin' jerkoff!" the driver screamed.

Nicholas ignored him. He looked up and down the street as he hit redial and then hit it again. It was a cool night and there was no one out for a walk, no one who might know what to do. If anyone had been out, they would have thought him quite a sight, his clothes wet, a cellular phone to his ear, his briefcase swinging back and forth as he ran.

"Come *on*!" Christine yelled at the unconscious man. "Breathe, damn you! *Breathe!*"

A man's dying, Nicholas, he told himself. *Do something!*

Just then, he spotted a squad car coming toward them. He stepped back into the street, waving his arms wildly. The police car stopped and two officers got out warily. As Nicholas explained the situation to one, the other used the car radio to phone for paramedics. The first officer told him to wait by the lamppost, they'd be with him shortly.

84

Nicholas returned to Christine's side. He watched, help-less, as she struggled to save a stranger's life.

Some young boy's father? he wondered.

For the first time in a long time Nicholas Van Orton felt a sense of humility.

As paramedics and one of the police officers hoisted the man onto a stretcher, the other policeman stood with Nicholas and Christine. The young woman had managed to get the man breathing again just before the ambulance arrived. The EMTs were impressed. So was Nicholas.

"You'll have to fill these out," the officer said, holding out a wooden clipboard.

"But we don't know this man," Nicholas said.

"What do you need?" Christine asked.

"A full report of what you heard, saw, and did," he said.

"The man keeled over. Probably too much to drink or too much pork. What the hell does that have to do with us?"

"It may be as you say," the officer said. "But there are no other witnesses. If the doctors discover that there may have been an assault of any kind, there will be an investigation."

"Come on," Nicholas said angrily. "I don't have time to be involved with this."

"You're involved whether you want to be or not," the officer said. "We'll have to detain you if you refuse to cooperate."

"Detain me? On what grounds?"

"Obstruction of justice. Possible suspects in a potential criminal action. Take your pick, sir."

"Bullshit double-talk," Nicholas said.

"The law," the officer corrected him.

"Gestapo tactics," Nicholas replied.

"We're ready to move out!" one of the paramedics shouted.

"Ride with your wife in the ambulance," the police officer told Nicholas. "We'll meet you at the hospital."

"She's not my wife," Nicholas snapped.

"I pity the woman who is," Christine muttered as she climbed into the ambulance.

Nicholas followed her in. One of the paramedics shut the door. Nicholas put his briefcase between his legs and Christine placed the clipboard on top of her knees. She began marking off boxes. Nicholas dropped the waiter's check on top of the papers.

"What's this?" she asked.

"What I was trying to tell you about back in the alley. Fifteen minutes ago I was looking forward to a quiet dinner when I get this note. I shouldn't let you get away."

"I had a boyfriend's mother tell him that once."

"I'm serious," Nicholas said. "There's something going on that you don't know about."

"Yeah? What."

Nicholas held up a finger, telling her to wait. Then he looked at one of the paramedics and pointed to the man on the stretcher. "This guy's breathing, isn't he?"

"Yes, sir."

"Good," Nicholas said. "Then is the siren entirely necessary?"

"It is, sir," said the young man. "Those are the rules."

"Jeez," Nicholas said. "Everybody's got rights around here except me."

"Us," Christine replied. She handed Nicholas back his

check and resumed filling out her form. "I've decided I don't want to hear the story of what's going on that I don't know about," she said. "I just want to finish this and figure out what I'm going to do with the rest of my life."

Nicholas put the check in his inside coat pocket and sat back. It suddenly struck him, the paramedic's choice of words: "Those are the *rules*." Was all of this part of the Game?

The ambulance raced to San Francisco General Hospital in the Potrero district. The vehicle sped down a ramp, moved quickly through an underground garage, did a sudden U-turn, and backed up to a busy emergency room entrance. One of the paramedics opened the door. Medical personnel seemed to be everywhere as injured people were moved from other ambulances. Nicholas and Christine got out and stood to one side as the heavy man was carried off. They watched as he was rushed inside through a pair of automatic doors. Christine raised her eyebrows, turned to Nicholas, and handed him the clipboard.

"Your turn, Mr. Sensitive."

"I'm sorry?"

"Mr. Sensitive," she said. "Your poor ears. I never heard of anyone complain about a siren on an ambulance before."

"I was trying to tell you something important," Nicholas said.

"And they were trying to save someone's life," she replied. "But I guess that isn't important to a man like you."

"That's not fair," he replied. "I admire what you did."

"Save it."

He looked at the clipboard as she walked away. "Hey, you forgot your driver's license number."

"No, I forgot my license," she said as she headed toward the door.

"Where are you going?"

"To talk to whoever can get this over with."

"Hold on," Nicholas said, running after her.

Suddenly, all the lights in the garage went out. Nicholas froze. So did Christine; she was still close enough so that he could see her in the glow of the bulb from the ambulance. All around them footsteps were scattering, people silent.

"Aw, you've got to be kidding," Nicholas said.

"What's happening?" Christine asked.

"It's what I was trying to tell you," he said, moving toward her. "It's a game."

"A game?"

"It's run by a company," he said. "They play elaborate pranks. Things like this. I'm really only now finding out myself."

"Pranks?" she said. "What the *hell* are you talking about?"

"I'm talking about a kind of recreational activity which, apparently, throws some kind of mystery at you which you have to solve. The lights go out. A dozen or so people run away, leaving us alone."

"You mean we were brought here on purpose?"

"I was, anyway," Nicholas said. "And I guess I was supposed to bring you too. That's what the waiter's message meant."

"So then—you mean the guy who plopped down on the street, who turned blue and wet himself—"

"Probably a plant," Nicholas said as he reached Christine's side. "Someone to get us here, to this point."

"For what?"

"I don't know," he said. "I truly don't. I'm sorry."

"You should be!" she blasted him. "Mother Mary, listen to me! I'm sounding like you did back at the restaurant." She headed toward the ambulance, shaking her head.

"What are you doing?" Nicholas asked.

"There's got to be a flashlight in there. I'm going to find it and get the hell out of here—and away from you."

He watched as she climbed in the back and began opening and closing drawers. He pursed his lips. He didn't understand why they were involving her.

"Empty!" she hissed. "Well, what did I expect. This is so fucked." She climbed out, opened her purse, and pulled out a book of matches. "And to think, I thought that guy was gonna die. I gave him mouth-to-mouth. I pulled snotty crud from his throat."

"That probably wasn't real," Nicholas said helpfully.

"Yeah, great." She lit one of the matches. "See you around. Or maybe not. I'll bet we move in different social circles."

"Where are you going?"

"Home," she said. "I'll just follow the yellow brick ramp back to the street and make my way to the nearest bus stop."

"Let me go with you," he said.

"No, thanks," she replied. "Weird shit seems to follow you around." The match burned out and Christine struck another." She looked around. "Uh—you happen to remember which way we came in?"

"Not really, no. But then I'm guessing we weren't supposed to remember."

She stared at him in the flickering light. "Part of your stupid game, huh?"

He nodded. Just then Nicholas heard a *ping* in the distance. He turned just as an elevator door opened somewhere. "Christine—bring those here," he said. "The matches."

Christine hurried over. Nicholas took the book, lit a match, and shielded it as he started moving through tightly parked cars. He stepped around columns, Christine behind him, until they saw the lighted carriage. They hurried toward it.

"Motherfucking frat boys," she grumbled as they sidled through the cars. "You better hide, you little assholes."

Entering the modern, brightly lighted carriage, Nicholas

pushed all the buttons. Nothing happened. Christine opened the emergency phone door. The compartment was empty.

"This is unbelievable," she said.

"More than you know," Nicholas remarked as he noticed the key slot. With a flash of excitement he reached into his pocket and pulled out his key case. He flipped up the C.R.S. key and put it into the slot.

It fit. He turned the key. The doors closed and the elevator moved up. It was the first moment of satisfaction Nicholas had known all day.

"Okay," she said. "Do you want to at least *try* and explain?"

He faced her, trying to keep one eye on the floors as they lit up. They had been in sub-basement four when they started. "It's a long story, Christine. My brother Conrad hired this company called Consumer Recreation Services. They create what I guess are like mystery weekends—"

"Which are what, for the uninitiated?"

"Where you go to a resort or a convention and try to solve a fake crime."

"Like I said," Christine told him, "we move in different social circles."

"It's not important," Nicholas said. "This thing started when I found that key," he pointed, "in the mouth of a wooden clown in my hallway—"

"You know what?" she said. "Never mind. I've heard enou—"

Her jaw clapped shut as the elevator lurched and then stopped suddenly. The overhead lights went on and a red emergency light came on. Save for Nicholas's thudding heart and Christine's raspy breathing, the silence was absolute.

"Speaking of clowns," she said, "we should never have gotten in this elevator."

Nicholas pressed the red alarm button. It didn't work. He didn't bother pushing any of the other buttons. He had a feeling they weren't going to work. The floor numbers had stopped lighting up too; he had no idea where they were. He took out his cellular phone and tried it. He punched 911 and frowned. "Static."

"Why am I not surprised?" Christine said anxiously. She stepped toward the door and began to pound it. "*Hey!*" she cried. "*Anybody out there? Yo!*" She kicked it angrily. "So tell me. What's the going rate for a trapped-in-an-elevator adventure these days?"

"I'll have to ask Conrad if I ever see the bastard again," Nicholas said. It occurred to him just then—only because he was thinking about it now—that Conrad had never intended to show up for dinner. He must have phoned C.R.S. and they'd scheduled the Game to start with that goddamn waiter. As his eyes adjusted to the carmine darkness, he noticed Christine's eyes looking up.

Toward the trapdoor on the ceiling.

"Don't even think it," Nicholas said.

"Why not?" she said. "You have a better idea?"

"As a matter of fact, I do," he said. "Read the sign on the wall next to the alarm button."

Christine followed his finger.

"It says, *Warning. If elevator stops, do* not *attempt to exit carriage. Use the emergency phone—*"

"Which isn't there—"

"—and *wait for help,*" he continued. "Wait. For. Help. That's what I plan on doing."

"I see. And do you honestly believe that help is going to come? Do you think that whoever stopped this elevator is suddenly going to start it up again or send the cavalry?"

Nicholas stared at the woman for a long moment. *Of course someone would come for them,* he thought. Unless this was not a hospital and everyone had been paid to be there, hired like movie extras. In which case C.R.S. would send help in two or three days, after he and Christine had passed out from hunger.

Or maybe they won't send help, he told himself. Who knew? Maybe the people who went to C.R.S. for kicks were twisted damn people who *liked* danger. Real danger. Certainly Conrad fit that category. He was a guy who'd snuck down to a beach in Cuba when he could have bought a cheap ticket to Florida or Antigua or some other sunny patch of sand and surf.

Nicholas looked up at the door. What if it didn't open?

It had to, he decided. *They've led us by the noses this far.*

Taking off his jacket and handing it to Christine, he stepped on his briefcase and climbed onto the handrails. He reached up and pushed on the door. It creaked and then fell back with a thud. He peered up. It was darker than hell's night up there. Solid, flat black.

Nicholas hopped back down. "Tell you what," he said. "How about I give you a boost?"

"Uh-uh," she said adamantly.

"What do you mean?"

"I mean you go first. You're the guy."

"Listen, Christine, this isn't a matter of me being brave or not. I'm scared, just like you are. But I'm also being sensible. You're shorter than I am. If I don't lift you out, how are you going to get up there?"

"You're going to go up there, check it out, and then pull me."

"That's stupid. Me pushing you up will be easier. You step up to the rails, grab the edge of the doorway, and I give you a boost."

"No."

"Please?"

"No!" she said. She looked down. "I'm not wearing underwear. There. I said it. You satisfied?"

"Under ordinary circumstances I might be," he said. "But I'm way too tired to enjoy the view right now. Please reconsider."

She shook her head.

With a sharp, disgusted exhale, Nicholas climbed back onto the rails, stuck his arms through the opening, placed his palms onto the dusty top of the carriage, and pulled himself through.

chapter 16

The shaft was chilly and Nicholas asked Christine to throw his jacket up to him. After he slipped it on, he lit one of the matches and looked around. There were two metal guide rails on either side of the carriage. Just behind him were three thick, parallel cables. These vanished into the darkness above, to the pulleys that moved the elevator. He couldn't see the counterweight or the motor; he had no idea how high the top of the building was or where the next doorway was.

"See anything?" Christine asked.

"Nothing promising," he said. As he turned around, the match burned down to his fingertips. He shook it out and lit another.

And he saw one of the most beautiful sights he'd ever seen.

"I take that back," he said. "There's a ladder here."

"My hero," she said.

Through the sarcasm Nicholas could hear relief. That gratified him: she wasn't quite the iron lady she made herself out to be. He dropped to his knees beside the trapdoor. "Hand me my briefcase and then I'll pull you up."

Christine pushed the heavy briefcase through the opening then clambered onto the handrails. He pulled her by her forearms which afforded him a better grip. Moments later, with Nicholas in the lead, they were on the ladder and climbing up the shaft.

The climb was short and uneventful. Nicholas saw a vertical sliver of light about ten feet above and they headed toward it. He struck a match when they arrived. There was a handle on the left-side door, the side near the ladder. There was a lock which, when twisted, enabled him to open the door effortlessly. They climbed the ladder until they could swing easily onto the floor. They were in a vast lobby with a sky-lit atrium.

"Damn," Nicholas said as he wiped his greasy hands on his pants. "My briefcase."

Christine crossed her arms. "I'll wait."

He looked back down the shaft. "Well . . . it's not like anyone could actually open it."

"Or care what they found," she said. "I mean, your typical elevator maintenance guy just isn't going to care about high finance."

Nicholas sighed. She was right. Besides, the damn thing was battered all to hell. *Fuck it,* he thought.

They started through the deserted lobby. As they did, Nicholas grinned knowingly. "I should have known," he said.

"What?"

"This is C.R.S."

"What's C.R.S.?" Christine asked.

"This is. It's their building."

"The whole thing?"

"I'm beginning to wonder," Nicholas said.

Suddenly, an alarm sounded. Nicholas looked around and then up. Just above them he saw the red light of a motion detector.

"Well," he said, "at least now we'll get some help."

"What do you mean 'we'?" she asked. "I'm not a part of this."

"You are now," he said. "Sorry. But it's no big deal. When security gets here we simply explain what happened—"

"They'll love hearing it."

"I don't care whether they do or not," he said. "It's the truth."

Christine looked around the lobby. "You know what?" she said.

"What?"

She started running. "You can explain for both of us."

"Wait!" he said. "I don't think you should go anywhere until I make sure that this is the end of the Game!"

"Write and let me know!" she said as she sped around a corner.

Nicholas swore and started after her. Some of these buildings had patrol dogs which were let loose in shipping bays to protect equipment and supplies. And they didn't just bark at intruders.

He caught sight of Christine as she burst through a pair of *Emergency Exit* doors. Breathless, Nicholas arrived a moment after she did. They were on an outdoor loading dock. He gripped her arm tightly.

"First Dennis, now you," she complained. "I'm gonna be black and blue there."

"It could be worse," he said. "You could run into guard dogs or some green schmuck of a kid with a nightstick."

Christine's mouth clapped shut. Nicholas heard a car somewhere behind them but coming closer.

"Just walk slowly," Nicholas said. "Don't draw attention. We're out for a stroll."

"Mr. Grease Monkey and Ms. No Underwear with underarm sweat stains the size of a Great Lake," she said. "Just your average San Franciscans."

"There's worse," he said.

Tires screamed behind them. A spotlight threw their

shadows in front of them. A no-nonsense voice came over a loudspeaker.

"You two! Stay where you are."

Christine and Nicholas both looked back. The security car was on the other side of a chain-link fence.

Christine slipped her arm free. "Me?" she whispered to Nicholas. "I'm gonna run."

She did, hurrying up a ramp which ran alongside the building. Nicholas followed. If the Game was over, if the guard wasn't a part of it, he had no intention of trying to tell this story by himself.

The ramp turned into a narrow alley. Christine ran past it. Nicholas caught up to her and, together, they sprinted around a corner.

Just as a security car skidded toward them.

"Shit!" Christine cried. She doubled back.

Nicholas followed. "Where the hell are you *going*?"

She stopped beside the alley. It was little more than a two-foot space between the C.R.S. building and an old brownstone—a space which probably hadn't existed before the newer building replaced whatever had been here.

"You can't fit there!" Nicholas cried. Breathless, he stopped beside the alley. Christine was already edging through. "All right. *I* can't fit there."

There was another mechanical-sounding shout behind him as the two security cars bore down on him. With an oath, Nicholas took off his jacket, turned sideways, and began sidling through the alley. Despite the muscle-bottom bane known as "squash butt," Nicholas was doing surprisingly fine.

One of the cars stopped. A door slammed and a flashlight shined at Nicholas from the opening of the alley.

"You!" shouted the guard. "Come back."

Nicholas looked out at him. *Yeah, right,* he thought.

In the beam of the car headlight he saw the silhouette of the beefy security guard as he struggled to enter the alley.

He didn't get very far. In fact, he didn't even get in. Which is why he hurried back to the car, opened the back door, and let a German shepherd loose.

The dog wasn't too thick to fit in the alley. It shot between the walls like a missile gaining quickly on Nicholas.

He knew he'd never make it out in time. He looked up. There was just one chance. Bracing his backside against the wall behind him and digging his shoes and fingertips into the brick wall in front of him, Nicholas began climbing. He was about eight feet up when the dog arrived. It leapt at him but fell at least a foot short. Behind, Nicholas heard the guard urging his dog on. The second guard arrived and then disappeared. Ahead, Nicholas saw Christine pushing two plastic trash cans into the mouth of the alley, one atop the other.

Smart lady, he thought.

Somewhat relieved, even though he could still slip and fall into those snarling jaws, Nicholas began shimmying slowly toward the exit, about fifteen feet away. He reached it without further incident and managed to propel himself down and out, onto the other side of the trash cans. They were wedged in tight enough so that the dog couldn't get through.

Christine began walking down a larger side alley. Nicholas followed. There was a chain-link fence ahead with a gate.

"This should lead to Sansome Street," she said.

"That was good thinking, about the trash cans," Nicholas said admiringly.

"Thanks," Christine replied.

"Even though it was shitty the way you deserted me," he added.

"You're a grown man. I'm not responsible for you."

"You are when you start running and bring the wrath of the guards down on us."

"Me? Say, who's the one who got us *into* this mess to begin—" she stopped. "Did you hear that?"

"Just the dog," Nicholas said.

Christine turned slowly. "Shit."

Nicholas turned, too, just as the dog managed to knock the topmost of the two trash cans on its side. Though the plastic can was still wedged between the walls, the barrier was now low enough so the dog could reach the top. It bounded onto the upper can and jumped over.

Christine swore again and began running. Nicholas followed. She reached the gate but it was closed with a chain and padlock.

"Climb!" Nicholas cried as he helped her up the fence. He got himself a few feet up just as the German shepherd arrived. It leapt and got its teeth around his ankle. Nicholas screamed as his flesh and pants ripped. The dog fell back, its mouth full of cloth.

"Are you okay?" Christine yelled.

"Yeah, sure," he lied. His calf burned like hell from the bite.

They reached the top and swung over just as three more dogs came running at them from the street—two pit bulls and a Doberman pinscher. Nicholas cursed loudly. He knew now where the second guard had gone. As the four dogs barked and jumped, Nicholas and Christine straddled the top of the fence. They sat there, three feet apart, as though they were riding horses.

"Now what?" Christine asked.

"I'm open to suggestions," he said. He held on tight as the dogs threw themselves against the fence. He wasn't so much afraid of the guards anymore. He and Christine were cornered. Even if the two men had guns, they wouldn't shoot. In the morning the security office could check with C.R.S., find out just what Nicholas and Christine were doing here, and that would be that. What he was afraid of was falling and being mauled before the security people got there.

The Doberman hit the fence hard and Christine nearly tumbled over. Nicholas grabbed her belt and steadied her.

"Hands off, mister!" she said. She had to yell to be heard over the yapping dogs.

"Sorry," he said. "I meant to save your ass, not touch it."

She scowled. Nicholas looked away. As he did, he noticed something from the corner of his eye. Behind them, about twenty feet, the fence ran under the fire escape of an old building.

"I have an idea," Nicholas said.

"What?" Christine yelled back. She leaned down. "Shut up, you stupid fucking dogs!" She looked back at Nicholas. "What did you say?"

"I said I have an idea!" he shouted. "Follow me!"

Nicholas began sliding backward, glad that the links stopped below the top rail instead of above it. Christine followed, alternately looking back at him and down at the dogs.

"What the hell are they guarding here?" she asked. "Each other?"

"Y'know, I'm not sure they guard anything," Nicholas said. "I'm wondering if this is still part of the Game."

"And you paid for this privilege," she said, shaking her head. "You are one sick dude."

"I didn't pay for it," he said. "My brother did."

"Then *he's* one sick dude," she said.

"Let's not get into that."

"Or else he's got some kind of mad-on for you."

"Let's not get into that either," Nicholas added.

Thinking about Conrad and this stupid game caused Nicholas to kick the fence once with his heels. As he did, one of his loafers slipped off and the dogs vaulted up, as though it were a jump-ball. The Doberman snagged the prize and came down among the others. White teeth and spittle gleamed under a nearby street lamp as the three dogs tore at the shoe. The German shepherd pushed its muzzle through the fence in a futile effort to get its share.

"There goes a thousand dollars," Nicholas complained.

"Hold on. Your *shoes* cost a grand?"

"No," Nicholas said. "That one did."

Christine shook her head. "Two hundred dollars a toe," she said under her breath. "Those dogs never ate so well, I'm guessing."

Nicholas didn't disagree. He also reminded himself that if he lost his temper again, even for a moment, it might be his three-hundred-dollar shirt, seven-hundred-dollar pants, and quarter-billion-dollar butt that the dogs would be eating next. He concentrated on getting to the fire escape.

As soon as he reached the building, he got his knees up on the fence and turned sideways. He got his left foot on the top of the fence—the one that still had a shoe—then drew his right foot beneath him. He looked up. The bottom of the fire escape was about seven feet overhead, perpendicular to the fence. It was far enough out from the wall so that Nicholas couldn't lean on the wall for support. If he tried, it would hit him on the head as it came down. He also knew he wouldn't be able to balance himself on the top of the fence for more than a second. He was going to have to stand, reach up, and grab the fire escape in one fluid move.

The dogs finished up with the shoe and moved under him. There was still no sign of the guards; obviously they were part of the Game. He wondered if they would suddenly materialize if he fell.

He didn't want to find out.

He hunched down, let go of the fence, and shot up into a standing position. At the same time he reached up and grabbed a rung of the fire escape. It came down on the three-dog side of the fence. The animals immediately rushed over but were unable to get a paw-hold.

Holding onto the side of the ladder with one hand,

Nicholas extended the other hand back to Christine. She grabbed it, rose cautiously, and then sidled over. When she was near enough, she grabbed Nicholas's waist.

"Thanks," she said.

He looked into her eyes. They weren't exactly warm and inviting, but they were appreciative. It was the first non-hostile expression he could remember seeing in them.

"You're welcome," he said softly.

Together, they caught their breath for a moment and then began climbing.

chapter 17

I never got your first name," Christine said as they climbed the stairs past boarded-up windows.

"Nicholas," he said.

"Like the czar," she replied.

"No. He's dead. I'm not. I intend to stay that way."

They reached the top of the abandoned four-story building, crossed the roof, and descended the fire escape on the other side. Upon reaching the last landing, Nicholas stepped on the ladder to swing it down. It wouldn't move and he kicked it with his left foot.

"Must be rusted," he said.

"The ladder or your foot?" Christine asked.

Nicholas ignored her. He sat and kicked the ladder harder. It squealed—and dropped with a loud, echoing clatter to the alley below.

"You sure your name isn't Clark, as in Clark Kent?"

He stared at the ladder. She wasn't funny but everything else was a frigging joke.

"Or maybe this is *my* Game," Christine said thoughtfully. "Somebody who hates me bought it for me. Let's see. My father? And you're an actor or a ringmaster or whatever."

"I wish you were right," Nicholas said. He wanted to scream for these pricks to stop the whole Game. But somehow, he didn't think they'd listen.

Christine looked down around him, through the opening where the ladder used to be.

"There's a trash bin against the wall," she said. "Lid's shut—if we hang down here and drop, we could make it. It's only about ten feet."

"I think not."

"Why? Afraid you're going to ruin your one-and-a-half-legged suit?"

"No," he said. "I'm 'afraid' I've had simply enough." He sat back against the wall of the building.

"Well," she said, "it's gonna get pretty chilly up here and I have no intention of staying."

"I'll warm you."

"Thanks. But the only one Nick at night I'm interested in spending any time with is the one on the little TV in my studio apartment—which is where I intend to be before very much longer."

"So you can afford cable, huh?"

"Basic. It's a necessity." She got on her knees and turned her back to the opening in the landing. "You probably have a satellite dish with 152 channels, right?"

"Actually, it's 153 now. Last night I found out I've got the C.R.S. Network. Interactive TV. I don't recommend it."

"I don't even wanna know about it," she said as she grabbed the edge of the landing and lowered herself through.

Just as she was about to release the edge two young Oriental busboys threw open a door beside the bin. They used a brick to keep it from shutting. Then, oblivious to the woman swinging gently above them, they threw open the lid, hurled in a pair of overstuffed trash bags, and lit cigarettes. They leaned against the wall, smoking and chatting. The lid of the trash bin remained open.

One of the men looked up and blew smoke skyward. He stared and then pointed. The other young man looked up and they started laughing.

Christine looked down at her open, dangling legs. She gasped and tried desperately to use one hand to shove her skirt between her legs. As she did, she lost her grip.

Nicholas darted over and grabbed for her wrist. He missed and she landed in the trash bin, screaming as the bags exploded around her. Worried that she might have hurt herself, Nicholas dropped in after her. He managed to get his knees under him and helped her sit up.

The two busboys also ran over and extended helping hands.

"Christine, are you okay?"

"I'm okay, I'm okay," she said. "Get these perverts away from me!"

"They're only trying to help."

"Yeah, right," she snarled. She jerked her arms away from the busboys. "Hey, you want a view, go to Fort Point."

The men stepped away, confused. Nicholas hopped from the bin and then helped Christine out. She grunted and moaned a little as she climbed out, but she never took her eyes off the two busboys and she always kept her dress between her legs.

"You sure you're all right?" Nicholas asked. There were cuts on her arms and legs.

"Except for my bruised modesty," she said, glaring at the busboys.

"It'll heal," Nicholas said.

They brushed themselves off as the busboys watched.

Nicholas smiled at her as he plucked a piece of lettuce from her shoulder. "Mademoiselle," he said as he offered her his arm.

She smiled back at him and, together, they walked toward the door. Nicholas pulled it open and they entered the kitchen. Cooks, busboys, dishwashers, and waiters stopped what they were doing and looked over.

Nicholas saw one of the cooks preparing *me grob*. "Do you like Thai food?" he asked Christine.

"Love it."

"Excellent." He looked at the nearest dishwasher. "Two for dinner," he said cheerfully.

chapter 18

Nicholas and Christine walked east along Clay Street eating *pad thai* and *me grob* from plain white containers.

"I think we should file a discrimination suit," Christine said after a long and thoughtful silence. "It's not like Thai-Land is the City Club. Why shouldn't they have seated us?"

"Could it be the way we're dressed?"

"Why? You're wearing a jacket. Only the back of my bra is exposed. What's the prob?"

"It could be my missing pant leg, bleeding calf, one-shoe look," Nicholas contributed around a mouthful of noodles. "Or maybe it's the fact that we smell like a Dumpster."

"Half the people who go to dives like that smell like garbage. Half the food does too."

Nicholas smiled at her. "Somebody's feeling a little testy."

"No duh," she replied.

Nicholas was still smiling. He was sore as hell and his leg hurt from the dog bite but he was glad to be back in control of things. "You'll feel better when we get cleaned up."

"Is that what we're doing? A little late-night dip in the Transamerica fountain?"

"Not exactly," he said.

"Where, then?"

Nicholas pointed toward the Financial District skyline just two blocks away. "That tall, bright building. Right near there."

As they walked, a police car moved from behind them. Nicholas turned as a police officer shined a flashlight up and down.

"Everything okay, miss?"

"Yeah," she said. "How are you, Officer?"

The light snapped off. The squad car drove on.

"Glad they're on the job," Nicholas said.

"Yeah, now," she said. "Where were they when we were being mistaken for chew toys?"

They reached the Van Orton Group building in ten minutes. Nicholas still had his key case—including the damn C.R.S. elevator key, which he felt like chucking out the window—and they went up to his private office.

"There's a shower in the back," he said as he turned on the lights. The switch also illuminated the lights above his Monet, Cezanne, and Delacroix.

Christine walked ahead of him and peeked in. "A shower in your office? You an athlete or something."

"I'm an 'or something,'" he replied. He didn't feel like showering now. He was afraid that once he got in he might never want to get out. Instead, he went over to the closet and took out a new shirt and trousers.

"What exactly *do* you do?" Christine asked.

"Investment banking," Nicholas answered. "Moving money from place to place."

"Hmmm," she said. She walked over to the window and peeked through the closed blinds. "Sure pays better than moving dinner plates from place to place. Nice view."

"Huh?" He took a sweatshirt from the closet and walked

to her side. He looked over her shoulder. Then he glanced down at her neck. "Oh, yes. Yes. Terrific view." He held out the Penn State sweatshirt. "Care for a clean shirt?"

She accepted the shirt and frowned. "I'm a UCLA gal myself," she said. "Actually, I dated a guy who went there. That's as close as I got to school." She walked toward the bathroom, shaking her head. "I've gotta tell ya, Nicholas. If this was my office, I wouldn't keep the blinds closed."

"Yeah, well, I don't spend much time looking out the window. Besides, these paintings are pretty valuable. Sunlight would cause them to fade."

"Then take them down and put plants on the wall instead. Sunlight's good for them. And for you too."

She stepped into the bathroom but only partly shut the door. She faced the mirror. Nicholas watched as she took off her filthy shirt and dropped it in the wastebasket. He stared at her shapely, unblemished back and red bra. When she turned around, he averted his eyes, suddenly embarrassed. He didn't spend much time looking at women, either. But when he made the time he was reminded of how very much he enjoyed it.

"I'll call you a taxi," he said, clearing his throat. "Company account—my treat."

"Thanks."

Nicholas picked up the phone. Five minutes later they were back downstairs, bidding good evening to the night watchman as they walked toward the street and the waiting taxi.

"I know the owner of the City Club," Nicholas said. "I'll talk to him in the morning, get your job back."

"Thanks," she said, "but don't. It was a shitty job anyway and I've been there way too long. It's time for a change."

He opened the door for her and she sat down. Nicholas stood while she swung her long legs in.

"Good night, Christine," he said when she was inside.

"By the way," she said, "only my dad and that asshole Dennis call me Christine. My friends call me Christy."

Nicholas smiled. "Good night, Christy. It was nice meeting you."

"Likewise. If you give me an address, I'll send your shirt back."

"Keep it," he said. "A memento of an unforgettable evening." He shut the door and stepped back.

Christine rolled down the window. "Nicholas?"

He waited.

"I have a confession to make."

He felt his belly tighten. "Oh?"

"Back at the City Club? Someone gave me four hundred dollars to spill drinks on you as a practical joke."

He looked down at her. "Seriously?"

She nodded once.

"What did they say?"

"They said three hundred. I said four."

"No—I mean about me."

"They ordered the drinks and when I brought them they offered me the money and said I was to spill them on the guy in the gray flannel suit."

"And you just said yes?"

She grinned. "No. I said, 'You mean the attractive guy in the gray flannel suit?'"

Still grinning, she rolled up the window as she gave the driver her address. Nicholas watched as the taxi pulled away from the curb. It didn't matter, he realized, who had paid her. Probably Feingold or one of the C.R.S. flunkies. What mattered was the stab of regret he felt. He was going to miss the plucky Christy. However, contrary to what Dallas-man had said and contrary to what Conrad may have thought, he was not going to miss this night.

The Game was not for him.

Nicholas had the night watchman call him a cab to take him back to the City Club. There, he collected his BMW and drove home. After a long, very hot shower, he sat on his bed and clicked on the TV. He switched off CNN—it would be a while before he could watch it without his spine creeping—and surfed through a succession of infomercials, old movies, new movies, made-for-cable movies, and cartoons. He finally stopped when he caught sight of Bugs Bunny. He plumped up a pillow, lay back, and fell asleep to the tunes of *What's Opera, Doc*?

The beep of the cordless phone snapped him awake. He grabbed it from the night table before he was fully awake.

"Hel-hello?"

"Mr. Van Orton, it's Maria."

Maria . . . Maria. The office Maria. "Hi. Hello." He scooted up against the headboard.

"I . . . I thought I should call."

"What time is it?" he asked, still groggy.

"Eleven A.M. I took the liberty of rescheduling your nine A.M. with Allison and Dietrich. Are you . . . not feeling well?"

"Long story. I'm fine. I'll be in in an hour. And Maria, I left my briefcase at Ten Nineteen Montgomery. Check with their lost and found."

"I will. Also, Mr. Van Orton—Anson Baer is in town."

"Really?"

"Yes. He's staying at the Ritz-Carlton. He's requesting dinner tonight."

Nicholas rubbed his face. Peace conference, concession speech, or declaration of war? he wondered. "I'll let him know," Nicholas said. "Anything else?"

"One thing more. The Hotel Nikko called to say they have your American Express card at the front desk. You left it last night."

Nicholas swung from his bed and pulled his filthy jacket up from the bathroom floor. It was ripe with the smells from the night before. He got out his wallet and fingered the empty plastic pocket.

"Should I send someone?" Maria asked.

"No. Give me their number."

Maria did. Nicholas told her he'd see her in a while and hung up. Then he punched in the hotel number.

"Hotel Nikko," said a silky-voiced operator.

"This is Nicholas Van Orton. I'm told my American Express card—"

"Yes, Mr. Van Orton. We have it and everything's in order. The concierge has arranged for the wine and flowers in the room."

Nicholas looked around the drape-darkened room. "Has he?"

"He has. And a young woman phoned just now to say she's en route but running a little late."

"I see. Did this young woman leave her name?"

"No, sir. She did not."

"Thank you," Nicholas said and hung up.

Forty-five minutes later he was in his car headed to the Hotel Nikko—and trying, once again, to get Conrad on the phone. If this was still part of the Game, he wanted the whole thing stopped.

"There's no answer," said the switchboard operator at the Sheraton Palace. "Would you like his voice mail?"

"No, thanks," Nicholas said. "Just tell him his brother called and to call back as soon as he can." He gave her the numbers of his cellular and car phones.

"I'll give him the message, sir," the operator said.

Nicholas disconnected the phone and hung up. He glanced in his rearview mirror. A beat-up black sedan had been following him since he swung onto Washington Street a few blocks from his home. He couldn't make out the faces of whoever was in the car, they were too far back. But he had made a pointless round-the-block detour to Jackson Street just to see if they stayed with him, and they did. The Game was still afoot.

Upon reaching the Hotel Nikko, Nicholas left his car with the valet. A doorman opened the glass door for him. Nicholas removed his sunglasses and looked around for the registration desk. As he did, a thin man in a tan suit and a big hurry bumped into him.

"Sorry," said the man, without pausing. "My fault."

Nicholas watched as the man continued out the door. He didn't look back. Was that anything? He felt for his wallet. It was still in his inside suit pocket. Not everything had a sinister purpose, he decided. It only felt that way.

Spotting the registration desk, Nicholas walked over.

"Ah, Mr. Van Orton," the assistant manager said as he walked over. "Here you go." He handed Nicholas his American Express card.

Nicholas looked at him. "Have we met?"

"I believe we have," he said and smiled. "If you would just sign here." He pushed over a charge slip and handed Nicholas a pen.

Nicholas signed. He regarded it as a poker ante. The price of staying in the Game, whether he wanted to or not.

The assistant manager tapped a bell on the desk. An eager young bellhop appeared at Nicholas's side.

"Show Mr. Van Orton to his room," said the assistant manager.

Nicholas held out his hand. "The key?"

"I beg your pardon?"

"I'm sorry. Didn't I give you two?"

"No," Nicholas said. "You didn't."

The assistant manager seemed perturbed. Nicholas decided to check. He slipped his hands into his pants pocket, his jacket pocket—

There was a gold key in the right-hand pocket. Nicholas glanced back to the front door. The man-in-tan, of course.

"Cute," Nicholas said to himself.

The bellhop took the key. "My name is John. Any luggage, sir?"

Nicholas shook his head. He followed the young man, shaking his head no to the bellhop's Is-this-your-first-visit-to-the-Bay-Area? question and tuning out as the young man recommended new restaurants which weren't new but paid the chain or John to give them a plug.

The bellhop brought him to the second floor and led him down a long hallway to room 277. He went to put the key in.

"I'll take it from here," Nicholas said, folding a five-dollar bill into the young man's hand and then putting the key in the slot.

He turned it and opened the heavy door.

The drapes were drawn and it was dark inside. He turned on the hall light and saw a room service cart. There was wine chilling—the wine arranged by the concierge. Nicholas edged around it and continued down the short hallway. He turned on the room light. His mouth froze shut.

The large room had been totally trashed. The drapes were shredded, the TV had been smashed in, the drawers had been pulled from the dresser and broken, and the mirror over the bed had a spiderweb break across its entire surface. The room's two armchairs had been overturned and slashed and the king-size mattress had been stripped and cut down the center. The covers, sheets, and pillows had been ripped up and strewn around the room.

In the center of the ruined mattress sat Nicholas's briefcase. The latches were open but the lid was shut. Nicholas walked over and lifted it. He looked inside.

There was a stack of color photographs, eight-by-tens showing blurry sex acts. He thumbed through them. There were bodies in motion, limbs entwined, bare breasts. Deeper in the batch were pictures of a naked woman tied to the bed. Of two women with a nude man sandwiched between them. In all the photos only one face was visible: Nicholas's.

The photos looked about a year old, judging from his longer hair. They were computer cut-and-paste. He had no idea what they'd be used for—who gave a shit what he did in his private life?—though he realized it would probably be difficult for him to lead a stockholder's meeting or proxy battle the day after his bare butt (or what someone thought was his bare butt) had shown up in shareholders's mailboxes or downloaded from http://www.nicholasscheeks.

A loud knock at the door caused him to jump. He dropped the pictures on the bed, scurried over, and peered through the peephole. The maid was getting out her keys. She knocked again.

"Maid service!" she said.

Jeez, Nicholas thought as he fumbled to put the security chain in place. He slid it in just as the door opened—and stopped.

He looked through the opening. "Could you come back later?"

"Yes, sir," she said. "I'm very sorry."

"No problem," he said pleasantly.

The maid moved away. Nicholas shut the door. He went back to the room, shoved the photos back into his briefcase, and closed the latches. He turned and noticed a small, broken mirror on the desk with lines of cocaine on it. Swearing, he put his briefcase down, carefully picked up the mirror, and brought it into the bathroom. He ran it under the sink, his hands trembling.

The Game had never been amusing but now it was getting damned scary. *How far would these people go?* As he washed the mirror off, he accidentally cut his thumb on a jagged edge. He cried out and dropped the mirror, which shattered on the floor.

Aw Christ, he thought as he put his thumb under the faucet. After a moment he wrapped it in a washcloth, picked up the large pieces of glass, then grabbed a wad of tissues to wipe up the drops of blood on the sink and floor. He dropped the tissues in the toilet and flushed. The toilet burped as the water swirled and rose and kept on rising until it spilled over the rim and onto the floor.

"Jesus Christ!" he cried. "*Enough!*"

Backing from the bathroom, Nicholas grabbed his briefcase, opened the door, and looked down the hallway. He saw a maid cart to the left, heard a vacuum cleaner somewhere beyond it. The stairwell was to the right. He could get there without being seen. Slipping into the hallway, he shut the door and ran-walked to the stairs.

Two minutes later he was back in the lobby, heading toward the street.

chapter 20

Nicholas retrieved his BMW from the valet. Slipping on his sunglasses, he checked in his rearview mirror as he joined the thick morning traffic. The black sedan was back, two cars behind.

Nicholas wove through traffic and took a corner sharply. He sped through a yellow light and took another corner sharply. He slowed. A minute later the black sedan was right there again, two cars away.

"This is fucked," he said. There was an alley up ahead and he swung into it fast, as though he were going to try and get away. Instead, he stopped suddenly, got out, and stood with his back to the passenger's-side wall, where he wouldn't be spotted.

The black sedan swung in behind him. The driver had to brake hard to avoid a collision. When he did, Nicholas ran between the cars and pulled open the driver's-side door. The plump, mustachioed driver seemed alarmed. Especially when Nicholas grabbed him by the front of his white shirt.

"What the fuck—!"

"Why are you following me?" Nicholas screamed. He shouted right in the man's face, at the top of his lungs.

"I don't know what the hell you're talking about!" the man replied. "I'm just driving."

"My ass you're just driving," Nicholas said. His eyes snapped to an open file on the seat beside the driver. In it was a photo of Nicholas along with a computer printout. Nicholas fought the urge to punch the man's face in.

The man fumbled to close the file. "Look, bub—what I'm doing is none of your goddamn business."

"You've got a fucking *dossier* about me, asshole! I'd say it's very much my goddamn business!" He gripped the man's shirt tighter, choking him. "Is Anson Baer behind C.R.S.? Is that what this is?"

"I don't know what shit you're talking, but you better back off, jack-off."

"Had I better?" Nicholas taunted.

The man moved his thick right hand inside his jacket. Nicholas saw the shoulder holster inside the jacket. Releasing the man, he slapped him to disorient him, then shot his arm across his chest. He grabbed the .38 but the gun didn't come out. Nicholas knew what to do: it was a police holster. You had to push down to get the weapon. Unlike other parties, he never missed the Police Benevolent Association functions. He liked having those people on his side, doing him favors and giving him little pointers. They came in handy.

Nicholas turned off the ignition and released the man. He pointed the .38 at his forehead.

"Hey!" the man shouted, throwing up his hands and recoiling.

"For horses," Nicholas said. He was perspiring, his teeth clenched, his temper taught. He couldn't believe that he was actually pointing a gun at a man. He usually went after people with lawyers. He had to admit, though, there was something very satisfying about this. "So tell me, tough guy" Nicholas went on. "Does the Game use real bullets?"

"What frigging *game*?" the man asked.

"The one I'm getting real tired of," Nicholas said. He suddenly turned and pointed the gun at the sedan's rear tire. He fired. The gun echoed through the alley, swallowing the loud, quick pop of the tire. He was surprised at how smooth the trigger was and how strong the recoil was. Delicacy and power in one sneeze-fast moment. He liked it.

He swung the smoking weapon back toward the man. But the driver had taken the opportunity of the tire's demise to scoot over to the passenger's seat and throw open the door.

"Fucker!" Nicholas swore as he ran around the back of the car. He caught the man before he could get away. The plump man dropped to his knees, his fat face shaking.

"Okay," the man said. "I'll talk . . . I'll talk. Wh-what do you want to know?"

"Well, I've already answered the first question. The Game does use real bullets. The second question is, Who the hell are you?"

"I'm a private investigator."

"You suck. I saw you since we left the Heights. Why were you following me?"

"Somebody hired me to keep tabs on you."

"Who hired you?"

"I-I don't know."

"Then how'd you get paid?"

"There was money with the dossier. It was slipped under my office door."

"How much money?"

"Three hundred bucks."

Same as Christine was offered. Nicholas wondered if that were significant or if that was simply the going rate for ballbusters.

Nicholas was about to take the dossier when he heard a police siren from down the street. Someone must have heard the shot and reported it. The last thing he wanted was to get caught. All of this would be very difficult to explain, even for a friend of the SFPD.

Sneering at the fat man, Nicholas ran for his car as the private eye got up clumsily and ran for the street. Jumping into the BMW, Nicholas shoved the gun into the glove compartment and gunned the car down the alley. As soon as he was on the street, he picked up his cellular phone.

Maria answered. "Mr. Van Orton's office—"

"Maria," Nicholas said, "have Sutherland meet me at the Ritz-Carlton."

"Mr. Van Orton!" she said. "We've been worried about—"

"I'm okay. Just do what I asked. I'm on my way there now."

"May I tell him—"

Nicholas disconnected the phone. He dropped it on the seat.

Fear was turning to rage. This wasn't a challenge. This was a fucking-with. It was payback of some kind. Conrad wouldn't have let a "game" get this far—killer dogs and incriminating drugs in a hotel room and loaded .38s. This had to be Baer's work. And if it was, the prick was going to pay.

Big time.

chapter 21

Sutherland's office was within walking distance of the Ritz-Carlton, on California Street. He rose as Nicholas entered. Nicholas didn't stop as he strode through the ornate lobby with its crystal chandeliers and eighteenth-century oil paintings. The attorney fell in beside him.

"You look terrible," Sutherland said. "What's happened?"

"Just follow me," Nicholas said.

"I assume we're seeing Anson Baer."

Nicholas nodded.

"I took the liberty of getting the room number from Maria."

"I figured you would," Nicholas said as they entered the elevator.

They got off on the third floor and headed to Baer's suite. A waiter was just rolling out the room service cart. Nicholas pushed past him with Sutherland in tow. The waiter shouted after them and Nicholas told him to go fuck himself. Sutherland turned and apologized.

Anson Baer looked up from the splendidly set table, startled. So did his wife and a woman in her early twenties.

"Nicholas," Baer said warily. He rose. "This is unexpected."

Nicholas opened his briefcase on the bed. He slapped the photographs down on Baer's western omelette. "Do you actually believe that because we publish children's books, anyone's going to care about my reputation?"

"Father?" the younger woman said.

"It's all right, dear," her father cooed.

Attractive, white-haired Mrs. Baer put her arms around their daughter's shoulders and hugged her close while Anson Baer dropped his napkin on top of the photographs. He rose.

"I don't know what you're talking about, Nicholas," the publisher said quietly. "In any case, why don't we step into the hallway?"

"Up yours," Nicholas replied. "You could have pictures of me wearing nipple rings and butt-fucking Captain Kangaroo. All anyone would wonder was whether the stock was up or down."

Sutherland lay a hand on Nicholas's shoulder. "I think you'd better calm down, old friend."

"I think you better shut up," Nicholas said without turning around. "I'm not finished." He continued to glare at Baer. "The fact that you've involved Conrad is unforgivable."

"I still don't know what you're talking about," Baer said. "But if you're quite finished—"

"Not yet," Nicholas snarled. "This is my attorney, Samuel Sutherland. I thought you two should meet."

"We did meet," Baer replied. "This morning."

Nicholas looked at Sutherland. The lawyer nodded.

"I signed the termination contract for Baer/Grant," Baer said. "I accepted your settlement, Nicholas."

Nicholas felt light-headed as the rage burned off, replaced by an unavoidable tide of stupidity.

"You were right," Baer continued. "I'm going sailing.

You're welcome to join our luncheon this afternoon. Maybe we can straighten all this out." He indicated the women sitting across the table. "You remember my wife, Mary Carol, and my daughter-in-law Kaliegh."

The two women mumbled their greetings. Kaliegh made an effort to be pleasant. Mary Carol did not. Nicholas just stood there.

"It seems," Nicholas said. He stopped, took a breath. "It seems I've— Please, I hope you'll disregard my apparently misguided remarks."

He picked up his briefcase. He looked at the sad-faced Sutherland and then at the waiter, who had remained in the open doorway. Under the glare of five pairs of angry eyes Nicholas felt as if he were moving in slow-motion. He couldn't get out of the room fast enough.

Behind him, he heard Sutherland say to the Baers, "It was very nice meeting you all. I hope you enjoy your lunch."

Nicholas stopped in the hallway. He looked back into the room, feeling mercifully invisible. He watched as Sutherland stepped over to the publisher's plate and retrieved the soggy photographs. He bundled them in the napkin then turned toward the waiter.

"Young man," he said, "please bring Mr. Baer another omelette. Mr. Van Orton's treat."

Sutherland looked at Nicholas. Nicholas did not object. The attorney handed the waiter his business card. "Call to arrange payment."

With that, the attorney followed Nicholas out the door.

The men walked to the lobby in silence and Nicholas drove to his office in a deep, blue fog. He was sad, humiliated, and confused. If Anson Baer wasn't behind this, who was? How could it be stopped? Conrad probably knew the answers to both questions but Nicholas couldn't get in touch with him.

He was still in a dark mood as he arrived at his office. He ignored Maria as he walked in and shut the door. He sat behind the desk, his head in his hands. Sutherland arrived a minute later. He entered unannounced.

"Well, Nicholas," he said. "How concerned should I be?"

"About what?" Nicholas said. "The photos or my sanity?"

Sutherland sat across the desk from him. "Both."

Sutherland put the photographs on the desk. He opened the napkin and began thumbing through the pictures. "It does look a lot like you."

"You should see what they can do to the nightly news."

"What who can do?"

"It's complicated," Nicholas said. "Listen, can I ask a favor?"

"You know you can."

"I want you to find out about a company called Consumer Recreation Services."

"Find out what?"

"Everything," Nicholas said. "They're behind these pictures."

"Sounds like they make tennis rackets," Sutherland said. "What do we know about them?"

"Just the name," Nicholas replied.

"Nothing else?" Sutherland asked.

Nicholas suddenly held up a finger. "Wait a second," he said, and pulled open a large drawer in his desk. "Maybe." He pulled open a file folder and handed it to Sutherland. "When I signed all their papers—"

"You signed papers without me looking at them?"

"Like I said, it's complicated. Anyway, they gave me their waiver. See if that tells you anything."

As Sutherland opened the envelope, Nicholas pulled his briefcase onto the desk. It occurred to him that he hadn't looked past the photos back at the Hotel Nikko. He wondered if they'd put anything else in there.

They had. A business-sized envelope with a smiley face drawn on the front and a silver-plated metal crank. He examined the crank first. It was a handle of some kind, like an old tire jack.

"What is this?" Sutherland asked.

Nicholas looked up. "I told you. A waiver."

Sutherland handed over the pink-tinted paper. Nicholas examined it. Except for his signature and initials in several places, the page was completely blank.

"I can't believe it," Nicholas said. "Disappearing ink."

"You're joking," Sutherland said. "Someone is."

"Not me," Nicholas said. "It's what they do. I'm being toyed with by a bunch of"—he threw the pink paper at the stack of photographs—"by a bunch of depraved children."

Sutherland sighed. "Very well. I'll look into this C.R.S. And if you tell me I don't have to worry about these . . ." He indicated the photos.

"You don't."

"Fine," Sutherland said. He rose and turned to go.

"Sam?" Nicholas said.

Sutherland turned back. "Yes?"

"Thank you."

Sutherland smiled warmly then left. He shut the door behind him. Sighing, Nicholas tossed the pink paper into his briefcase, placed the crank on top of it, and pulled over the photographs. He began looking through them more carefully than he had before. Maybe there was something in them, a clue about the identity of the people, the place or places—

"Whoa."

He stopped at one of them. There was a shot from behind a woman's shoulder and neck, which filled most of the image. Nicholas was looking up from the bed, smiling. The unbroken mirror was behind him. In it, he saw the fuzzy, flash-clouded shape of what appeared to be a red bra.

He punched his telephone intercom. "Maria?"

"Yes, Mr. Van Orton."

"The other night—Jeez, it was last night—there was a

woman here named Christine. I called a taxi from that company we use—"

"Elite?"

"What?"

"Elite Taxi Company?"

"Yes. Look into it. Find out which car answered and where they took her."

"Will do," she said.

Nicholas sat back and steepled his hands, but only for a moment. He looked at the crank and picked it up. He put it in his jacket pocket. If there were one thing he'd learned in the past two days, it was this: if they give you something, you're going to need it.

Nicholas skipped lunch—and Anton Baer's luncheon—and managed to catch up on some of the work he'd ignored this morning. It was good to be back in the saddle again, doing something he enjoyed—and understood. He left shortly after dark and enjoyed the leisurely drive home. The ride was mercifully without incident and without anyone tailing him.

Upon pulling up to the garage of his estate, Nicholas took the precaution of removing the gun from the glove compartment and placing it in his battered briefcase. He looked around as he left the car, then walked briskly toward the house. Not that inside was any safer than outside, though he would feel less vulnerable in a bright, enclosed area. His muscles were beginning to ache from all the activity the day before and he was hoping he could have a long sit in the hot tub.

Just like Wyatt Earp, he mused. Just like in the days of the infamous Barbary Coast, having a bath with a gun at his side.

As he neared the kitchen door, Nicholas heard the distinctive *beep-beep-beep* of the telephone off the hook. He paused and put his face to the sliding glass door, cupping his hands around it to block the overhead spotlight. It was dark inside. Except for the glowing green numbers on the microwave and oven, he couldn't see a thing. He tugged on the door handle. It was unlocked and the slider opened. He entered warily.

"Ilsa?" he called as he stepped through.

There was no answer. Nicholas stood for a moment in the darkness, listening. Then he reached to the right to turn on the light.

He jumped and swore as blue sparks flashed. His hand and forearm tingled uncomfortably for a long moment; he bent close to the light. The switch plate had been removed, the wires exposed. Nicholas drove his palm into the wall beside it. Then he squatted and opened his briefcase. He took out the gun. He hung up the phone and walked toward the adjoining dining room.

"Ilsa?"

He stopped. The living room was the next room over and there was someone sitting there. They were in a chair in a dark corner, just outside the glow of a healthy fireplace fire. Nicholas raised the gun hip-high and approached.

"Who's there?" he asked.

There was no answer. He came closer. He could see, now, that it was the clown. He could also see a glossy, eight-by-ten black-and-white photo in its teeth. He pulled it out and turned toward the fire.

The browning photo showed Nicholas's father, his body sprawled on the ground. There was a paper clip on top and Nicholas turned the picture over. A red stamp on the back said *PROPERTY SFPD*. The paper-clipped, typed note beside it said, *Like my father before me, I choose eternal sleep*. There was a red signature arrow stuck beside a line at the bottom. The arrow said, *Sign here*.

Nicholas jumped as all the downstairs lights came on. The fixtures had all been fitted with black lightbulbs and only now did he notice that the walls, furniture, and drapes had been spray-painted with fluorescent graffiti. He turned a complete circle as he read.

Welcome home. Fuck you. Nicholas Van Cocksucker. Suck it. C.R.S. Rules! Having Fun, Rich Boy? The writing was a wavy, unbroken, multicolored line. He looked up. In the center of the ceiling it said, *Momma's Boy,* surrounded with various obscenities. He looked down. Ladders lay on the floor along with empty spray cans.

"Fuckers," Nicholas muttered. "*Ilsa!*" he shouted.

Feeling the weight of the gun, he turned toward the staircase and started up the carpeted steps. He followed the spray-painted words *Helter skelter* to the second floor. The fixtures here had also been fitted with black lightbulbs. There were more curses, more vile slogans, more hate-filled words spread across the walls.

He checked each room. The writing no longer had any impact. It was overkill. This whole damn thing was overkill.

He glanced out the window overlooking the kitchen. He saw the guest house, saw that the light was on. Retracing his steps slowly—he didn't want to be surprised by some asshole lurking around a corner—he headed outside. Walking swiftly to the guest house, he rapped on the door. An eye appeared at the peephole. A moment later the door opened.

The usually unflappable Ilsa stood there in her robe looking surprised. "Mr. Van Orton!"

"Ilsa. You're all right."

"Yes, certainly. What do you mean? What's wrong?"

"Did the alarm go off?"

"No. Of course not."

"Then—you didn't see?"

"I don't know what you're talking about," Ilsa said. "What's happened?"

"There's been a break-in," Nicholas told her.

"*Mein Gott!*" she said, looking out toward the house.

"What I want you to do is lock this door and stay here. Even if you hear shots. Just stay where you are."

"I will," she said as he turned and ran away. "And please, Mr. Van Orton—be careful!"

As he crossed the moonlit lawn, he pulled out his cellular phone. He slowed to a quick walk as he punched in the numbers.

"Nine-one-one emergency," said a woman's voice on the other end.

"I need the police. There's been a break-in at my home."

"Understood, sir," said the operator. "Remain on the line and give me your address."

Nicholas entered the kitchen. He was still on the phone as he punched the security code into the alarm keypad. "Twenty-two ten Broadway," he said. "The biggest house on the street."

"Understood, sir. You said it was a break-in—"

"Yes."

"Are you sure they're gone?"

"I'm not sure," Nicholas said. As he finished entering the code, there was a beep. Nicholas straigthened, worried. That meant the system was switching to battery power—

An instant later the lights went out. The clocks in the kitchen went down. The house was in utter darkness. In the silence Nicholas could hear the beating of his own heart.

"Sir," said the operator, "are you sure there's not still someone somewhere in the house?"

Nicholas didn't answer.

"Hello?" said the operator. "Are you still there?"

Nicholas was about to answer when something pounded hard on the sliding glass door behind him. Nicholas turned. When he saw who was there, he cried out and dropped the gun.

Standing against the glass, looking haggard and scared in the moonlight, was Conrad.

chapter 23

Nicholas guided the BMW down the silent streets of Pacific Heights. He took the corners fast, heading downhill, moving from the residential area toward the more urban section of town.

Conrad had asked him to take them away from the house. He told Nicholas that that was all he'd say for now, and Nicholas had done as he'd asked. As they headed south along Webster Street, toward Japan Town, Nicholas got his first good look at his brother.

Conrad looked like hell warmed over. There were dark circles under his eyes and his cheeks were dirty. His hair was unkempt and his clothes looked as if he'd been sleeping in them. Though Nicholas was glad to see that his brother wasn't the one behind this thing—it certainly wasn't a "game" any longer—he was anxious to know who was.

"You going to tell me what happened?" Nicholas asked.

Conrad held a finger to his mouth. He pointed up. Nicholas slowed the car and looked where his brother was pointing. There was a small knob, like the top of a hat pin, sticking from the interior roof fabric. Conrad pulled it—and kept on pulling. The fabric tore as a wire came through.

"What is it?"

"A microphone," Conrad replied after snapping the wire. "They're methodical. They're nothing if not that."

"Who is?"

"C.R.S.," Conrad replied. "Who do you think?" The younger man shook his head slowly. "Jesus, to think what I almost got you into."

"What do you mean?"

"I mean I'm so fucked," Conrad replied.

Nicholas glared at him. "Connie, what are you saying? You're not making any goddamn *sense*!"

"I'm saying that they fuck you and they fuck you!" he practically screamed. "And just when you think it's over, that's when the *real* fucking begins."

"Slow down, Connie," Nicholas said. "Take a big deep breath. Start at the beginning."

"The beginning is, I heard about the Game from a friend almost a year ago. I did it. They chased my ass through London, lotta fun, nobody got hurt. But that's just the start, see. It doesn't stop. I paid the bill, gave 'em their money, but then it all started again. They won't leave me alone!"

"What are they doing to you?"

"What *aren't* they doing?" he asked, tears in his eyes. "I'm a goddamn human piñata."

"But I don't understand," Nicholas said. "Why would they keep the Game going after you paid?"

"Because then you pay them more to make it stop. Then more. I'm guessing that when I've got nothing left of my inheritance—or I'm takin' a dirt nap—they'll stop."

Nicholas gripped the wheel tightly. If they were still harassing Connie after a year, he couldn't begin to imagine how long they'd be after him.

Suddenly there was a loud boom and the wheel jerked in Nicholas's hand. He eased off the pedal and struggled to keep control of the car as it swerved to the right. Sparks flew from the tire's metal rim as it scraped asphalt. A few seconds passed before Nicholas was able to maneuver to the curb. He stopped. He could smell the burning rubber of the few shards still clinging to the rim.

"They did this," Conrad said.

"It's just a flat."

"How do you know?"

"Because they couldn't have known which direction we were going. Hell, I didn't even know. Now, get a grip on yourself. We're going to figure this goddamn thing out."

Conrad dragged a hand through his hair. "Okay," he said. "Okay."

"Now, I'm just going out to check on it," Nicholas said. "Sit tight."

Conrad nodded.

Nicholas gave him a reassuring pat on the leg and slid from the car. A few moments later he returned to the open door. "Make that one blown tire and one dead cellular phone," he said. "Must be in a bad area for signals."

Conrad glanced down at the car phone. He picked it up. From his expression, Nicholas could see that it was dead as well.

"You know how to change a tire?" Nicholas asked.

"No. You?"

Nicholas shook his head.

"Can't be too difficult, can it?" Conrad continued.

"After everything I've been through?" Nicholas smirked. "Piece of fucking cake."

"Well," Conrad said, "we better get to it. I don't think we should be out in the open like this."

Nicholas rubbed his temples. "Pop the trunk," he said. "Button's in the glove compartment."

As Nicholas walked around to the back of the car, Conrad opened the glove compartment. As he did, dozens of silver and gold keys spilled out. Conrad looked at them lying in the light of the open glove compartment. He picked several up. They were all stamped with the letters C.R.S.

"You bastard!" Conrad screamed. He got out of the car. "You cocksucking bastard!"

"What?" Nicholas said.

"You're part of this. *You're* doing all this!" Conrad threw a handful of keys at his brother.

Nicholas raised a knee and hands to protect himself as the keys clattered around him. "Hold on, Connie! I don't know what those are!"

"*Bullshit!*"

"Someone must have put them there!"

"Yeah, you! You're behind the whole thing, aren't you?"

"Connie, what are you talking about? You were the one who brought this to *me*!"

Conrad stalked toward him. "The keys are right here . . . right in your fucking car. The keys of the fucking C.R.S. kingdom!"

"Listen, man!" Nicholas said, pushing against Conrad's shoulders as he arrived. Conrad shook him off. Nicholas stood his ground until the men were practically chin to chin. "Listen to what you're saying."

"No!" Conrad said. "You're not going to control this conversation like you always do."

"Fine! Terrific! You control it. And tell me why I would do anything like what you're describing!"

"Because you resent me."

"Horseshit."

"Really?" Conrad said.

"You're being emotional. Think it through."

"Okay. Let's. It kills you that I'm living my life. That I'm having fun and excitement and you're not, you envious, dickless, *fuck*!"

"Lower your voice," Nicholas said.

"Why? Afraid someone's gonna witness a scene? It'll get in the papers, be bad for business?"

Just then, someone opened a door and looked out.

"Get the fuck in your house!" Conrad screamed. "Get the fuck back inside your house!"

The door shut. Nicholas grabbed his brother by the wrists. Conrad took a step back and tore free.

"Are you afraid someone's gonna find out you're some kinda closeted, manipulative control freak?"

"Man," Nicholas said, "what is wrong with you? What are you on?"

"Oh, I've got to be 'on' something to be mad at you? Well, I'm so sorry I don't live up to your high expectations, Nickie. The truth is I'll never be you. And the fact is I don't want to be you."

"This is what you always do," Nicholas said. "Push the responsibility off onto me. Brother, what you are and what you're doing are your choices. All I ever did was try to help you."

"Thanks a nutbag full. I don't need your goddamn help. No one asked you to play dad."

"No!" Nicholas screamed for the first time. "Don't you say that to me! Did I have any choice in it? Did I have a fucking *choice*?"

"Yeah!" Conrad shouted back. "You could have been Nickie, my brother. Just like you always were!"

Sobbing, Conrad bolted away suddenly, running toward a nearby park. Nicholas ran after him.

"Connie!"

Conrad disappeared through thick bushes, lost in the dark. Nicholas followed, slipping and falling downhill along a grassy incline. He rolled several feet and then came to a stop against a row of hedges. He got right up and pushed through the scratchy branches.

"Conrad!"

There was a concrete path ahead, winding through a bank of pay phones. His brother was nowhere to be seen. Just then, one of the phones started ringing. Then they all did.

"You sons of bitches!" Nicholas shouted, pressing his hands to his ears.

They kept ringing and it occurred to him then that maybe there was someone he needed to talk to on the other end of one. He ran over and snatched up the first one.

"Hello?"

"Flippy?" a woman asked. "Is Flippy there?"

Nicholas slammed the phone down. He picked up the next one.

"Hello?"

The recording said, "If you'd like to make a call, please hang up and dial. Then deposit—"

He hung up and the phones stopped ringing. He turned to go after Conrad, then stopped. Digging his wallet from his jacket, he found the valet ticket on which he'd written the C.R.S. toll-free emergency number. He entered it and waited. He got a busy signal. He slammed the phone down, picked it up again, and punched in the number.

This time it rang. He got a recording.

"We're sorry," said the female voice. "The number you have dialed has been disconnected or is no longer in service—"

He smashed the receiver against the side of the cubicle and let it drop, tore the ticket in half, then kicked the phone for good measure.

He stepped back.

"Connie!" he cried.

There was no answer.

Disgusted with everyone and everything, he stormed off, back toward the row of hedges.

chapter 24

Nicholas returned to the car and looked down at the flat tire.

No, he thought. *That's not a flat tire. It's a dead tire. Deceased.* He popped the trunk and found the jack. He looked at it, turning it over, then dropped it back in the trunk. He didn't have the time or interest to try to figure it out. Maybe someone on the block would call AAA for him.

He looked up just as a taxi came driving down the street. Nicholas waved it down. Shutting the car trunk, he used the remote to turn the car alarm on and climbed into the cab.

"Twenty-two ten Broadway," he said.

The driver nodded and hit the gas.

Nicholas leaned back. He couldn't believe that Conrad thought he was behind this. It would take a sadistic lunatic to mastermind something like this. He might be many things, but he wasn't that.

Well, he thought, *I guess that depends who you ask.* Anson Baer. Maybe Maria. Maybe Sutherland. Maybe even Connie. *Not everybody sees things the way you do, do they, Nicholas?*

Nicholas loosened his tie. He looked out the window. "You'll want Laguna Street, to the right."

The cab was coming at it quickly.

"Excuse me, driver," Nicholas said, "you're going to miss the turn."

The driver said nothing. He spun the car north on Laguna Street.

Nicholas was thrown against the door. He closed his eyes. Goddamn San Francisco cabdrivers. Drove like bums. This one looked like a bum—a familiar bum, now that he thought about it. But from where? Where had he seen a homeless person recently?

Only at the airport—

Nicholas opened his eyes to check just as the taxi sailed past Broadway. "Excuse me," he said, "you missed my street."

Once again the driver didn't answer.

"Hey, can you hear me? You missed my—"

Just then, Nicholas noticed the driver I.D. on the other side of the partition. It said California Regal Sedans.

C.R.S.

Nicholas's hands became fists and he pounded the partition. "No . . . no, no, no, *no*! Stop the car! Stop it now, I want to get out!"

The taxi halted at a light. Nicholas reached to his left, for the door handle, but there wasn't one. There was no window handle either, just empty holes. He pulled up on the door lock but it refused to give. The cab peeled out the instant the light turned green. It crossed Lombard Street headed to Bay Street.

Nicholas collected his wits. He leaned toward the partition again and spoke loudly but calmly.

"Listen, driver. I'm a very wealthy man. Whatever they're paying you, I'll double it. Only stop the taxi and let me out."

The driver looked in the rearview mirror. He smiled as he

turned onto Bay Street and headed toward the Embarcadero. Once there, the taxi sped up, heading for a wharf area.

With a parting smile into the mirror, the driver opened the door and leapt out, executing a perfect roll.

Nicholas's eyes widened and his hands became claws as he raked to open the partition. It was sealed shut. Frantic, he sat back and fumbled for the seat belt. He found both ends and snapped them around his waist just as the taxi went flying from the deserted pier. Nicholas screamed, shocked by the high, helpless sound of his own voice.

It was quickly drowned by the smash of the car as it hit the Bay. Nicholas was jerked forward, the breath slammed out of him. It was surreal, watching the dark waters become darker as the cab sank. It rocked gently, almost pleasantly from side to side as big bubbles burbled from under it, disbursing smaller ones which leaked from the hood and trunk.

Nicholas opened the seat belt and lay on his back. He heard water trickling in up front and tried to ignore it.

"It's a game. A game," he reminded himself.

He put his heels against the window and braced his hands on the door behind him. He pushed with his feet. The window didn't give. He tried again. Nothing. He sat up, trying to stay calm. The headlights didn't provide much illumination in the weedy, silt-filled water. He smelled the ocean, the dead things in the ocean, as it seeped in. His shoes were wet. The water began pouring in more steadily from under the dashboard and through an opening in the trunk.

He had to get out. He slammed the door with the heel of his palm. It didn't open. And then he suddenly remembered the thing in his pocket. The silver crank he had taken from his briefcase.

He bent close to the door so he could see, then he placed the crank in the hole where the window handle should have gone.

It fit. He felt good about that, though he realized how absurd that was: he was still sitting in a car under at least twenty feet of water, a car which was sinking deeper by the second. Taking a deep breath, he turned the crank counterclockwise. The window began to lower and the San Francisco Bay began pouring in.

Rather than fight the flood, Nicholas waited until the car was entirely flooded. Still holding his breath, he squirmed through the window and knifed his way to the surface. It took only a few strokes to get there, but he'd been holding his breath for nearly a minute and sucked down the air greedily. He treaded water as he caught his breath in deep, grateful gulps and then he looked around.

There were people on the wharf and he waved to them. They waved back. He began swimming toward them and then someone jumped in to help him. A big, burly, bearded teenager.

Arm-weary and drained, Nicholas was never so glad to see anyone in his life. The young man helped him to the pier, where they climbed to the applause of the crowd just as a police car arrived.

chapter 25

Two police cars pulled up in front of the C.R.S. building the following morning. Two uniformed officers climbed from the marked car. Two detectives, along with Nicholas and Sutherland, emerged from the unmarked car. They crossed the lobby and went to the twenty-first floor.

The office where Nicholas had registered for the Game was empty. Except for dust and trash which looked as if it hadn't been touched in weeks. There were wires hanging from the ceiling, cables poking from holes in the Sheetrock, and not a human footprint anywhere.

Detectives Nadler and Pace remained behind while the officers gave Nicholas and Sutherland a lift back to the Van Orton Group building. The detectives came by three hours later. Nicholas stood behind his desk, his hands in his pockets, his expression grim, while the detectives sat in armchairs and read from their notebooks. Sutherland sat behind them, on the sofa.

"Management for the building says that space hasn't been officially rented yet," lanky, black-haired Detective Nadler said. "The county recorder has no listing for 'Consumer

Recreation Services' or any derivation or variation thereof. Divers are looking for the taxi and as soon as they find it they'll pull the plates and vehicle identification number."

"Have you heard from your brother, Mr. Van Orton?" asked the blond-haired Detective Pace.

Nicholas shook his head. He'd tried calling him at the hotel when he got home but Conrad hadn't called back. He was deeply concerned.

"What about the house?" Sutherland asked. "Any clues there?"

"The graffiti was painted in an oil-based marine marking solution," Nadler said. "Illegal in the states."

"Not impossible to trace," said Pace, "but it'll take time."

"The photographs of Mr. Van Orton, the gun, the clown, the ambulance, the cable box, everything else—we're still waiting to hear from our people about those," said Nadler. "We're also looking at the keys Conrad found in your car and we're going over the car itself. That investigation will also take time." He shut his notebook and put it in the pocket of his trench coat. "Breaking and entering: that we have. Solid."

"Malicious mischief," added Pace, "vandalism, harassment—we've got that too. But at the moment, that's all we've got."

"Illegal surveillance?" Sutherland contributed. "Reckless endangerment?"

"Attempted murder," Nicholas added.

"No proof as yet," said Nadler. He regarded Nicholas. "Besides. You'll forgive me, but you did say you *hired* these people."

"That is irrelevant," Sutherland said dismissively. "He did not hire them to break the law. He hired them to create a fictitious scenario in which he played an active but not dangerous part. That is all."

Pace scratched his head. "Fine, Mr. Sutherland. I buy that. In the meantime, it's our job to let you know what we have.

And what we haven't got is a motive. Something which made these people, whoever they are, escalate your 'game' into something more."

"Something personal," Sutherland contributed.

Nadler rose. "You are who you are, Mr. Van Orton, so we know you're not making this up for publicity."

"Damn right," Nicholas said, "and I resent the implication."

"I'm sorry you feel that way," said Nadler. "But we've never dealt with anything quite like this and we want to be thorough. We're going to ask every question, explore every angle, even if you don't happen to approve. It's not just you we're worried about. There could be other targets, other victims."

"I understand," Nicholas said. "I'm sorry."

Nadler nodded. "Be appropriately cautious. All right?"

Nicholas grinned. "Yeah. I'd hate to be offed by a nonexistent company. Bad for my image as a corporate shark."

The cops didn't smile. Neither did Sutherland. But Nicholas thought it was clever.

The rest of the day was without incident. Nicholas had figured that that would be the case, what with the police investigating every facet of C.R.S. Whatever it took, he wanted and needed this breather. Being trapped in a taxi as it plunged into the Bay had been enough excitement for this week. He left the office at seven, drove his repaired BMW home, and sat down to dinner in the kitchen. He just didn't feel like eating in the library or watching CNN tonight.

Ilsa set his plate on the table. She'd made a smoked turkey sandwich with the crust cut off, surrounded by potato chips and carrot stricks. Thousand island dressing was on the side, as Nicholas liked it. He spread some on the bread, took a bite, and looked around. Drop cloths, paint cans, and brushes sat in a neat pile in the corner. They'd been delivered late in the day, after the police had completed their investigation of the site and had okayed the repairs.

"Who'd you get to do the painting?" Nicholas asked.

"Mr. Michaelson," she said as she got a glass from a cabinet. "He's the one who did the outside."

"I remember," Nicholas smiled. "The old hippie."

"Not so old," Ilsa protested. "Only fifty-three."

Nicholas smiled. "I meant *former* hippie. Not ancient." He took another bite of the sandwich. "Tell me, Ilsa. What was my father like?"

Ilsa filled the glass with milk and walked over. "What makes you ask?"

"I'm not sure," Nicholas admitted.

She set the glass next to Nicholas's plate. "All the time I've known you, you've never once asked about him. Why now?"

"He came to mind recently, that's all."

Ilsa moved away. She was silent as she put the milk and unused turkey back in the refrigerator. "The things I remember most are two. Your mother loved your father very much. And he worked too hard."

"Would you say that he was morose? I mean—"

"Sad? Serious, like you?" She sat down. "What I remember most was his manner was so quiet. So . . . slight. It was easy to spend time in a room and not realize he'd been there the whole time."

"But what did he *think*?" Nicholas asked. "What drove him?"

"I don't know," she said. "I think your grandfather did not pay him much attention. I think he wanted that. I do not know what drove him in the end. To do what he did. What happened—no one expected it."

Nicholas looked down at his plate. "I wonder how much of him there is in me."

"Not much, I think. You are part of things, you are aware of things. He was shut off in his own unhappiness."

"Did Mom worry about him?"

"Nobody worried about your father. Not because they didn't care but because it didn't help. He refused to change."

As she spoke, the phone rang. Nicholas felt a chill; he got up to answer it and was relieved when he heard Maria's voice.

"Mr. Van Orton," she said, "sorry to disturb you at home."

"That's okay," he was surprised to hear himself say. Usually he hated being disturbed during dinner. "What's up?"

"I found the address you wanted from Elite Taxi."

"Excellent," he said. He picked up a pen. "Shoot."

Half an hour later Nicholas was driving slowly around South Basin, looking for the address Maria had given him. He found the street and the row of lower middle class homes. He parked in front of a white house with a small lawn. He double-checked the number on the door. Then he stepped on the quaint porch, with its healthy flowers and peeling paint, and rang the doorbell. As he waited, he looked out at the street. There were a few older cars and a motorcycle parked along the curb, and a white van just outside the glow of a street lamp.

Watching him? he wondered. More likely doing a drug or gun deal. He hoped this paranoia wasn't going to stay with him for his entire life.

The door opened slightly and a young woman looked out over the chain. "Yeah?"

"Hello," Nicholas said pleasantly. "I'm Nicholas Van Orton. Is Christine—Christy in?"

"She's sleeping."

"Could you possibly wake her?" he said. "This is important."

From behind someone shouted. "Who is it, Amy?"

"A guy named Nicholas Vinorden? Vanardin?"

"Van Orton," he said clearly and with a smile. It usually

ticked him off when people didn't get his name, when they didn't listen. He looked around Amy and saw Christine looking down from the top of the stairs. She was wearing a pajama top and shorts.

"Nicholas," she said as she caught sight of him. "What are you doing here?"

"Can we talk?" he asked.

Christine started down the stairs. "It's okay, Amy," she said.

The door closed, the chain came off the latch, and the door swung in. Christine was standing there with an expression that was one-half pleased, one-half intrigued, with a sprinkling of surprise.

"Didn't think I'd ever see you again."

"Life is full of surprises," he said.

"I didn't think you'd let that sweatshirt go," she complained. "Much too cozy."

"That's not why I'm here," he said. "May I come in?"

"Sure." She stepped aside. Nicholas entered and she shut the door behind him. She latched it again.

The house had no front hallway, just the living room, a dining room to the right, and the stairs leading up. The place was furnished with what looked like tag-sale chairs, tables, and art.

No longer smiling, Nicholas reached into his jacket pocket. He handed Christine a color photocopy of one of the eight-by-tens he'd found in his briefcase. It showed him with the woman in the red bra.

"What can you tell me about this?" he asked.

"You oughta get yourself a better photographer."

"Is this you?"

She looked at it more closely. "Hmmm. Where'd you get this?"

"It was left in my hotel room. Well, not really mine. You're saying it's not you?"

"I think I would remember. Don't *you* remember who it is?"

He shook his head. "I wasn't there. It's a paste-up job."

"I see," she said. She handed it back. "What makes you think it's me?"

"The, uh—the red bra."

She raised an eyebrow. "How do you know I—"

"When you were changing in my office," he said. "I didn't mean to look, but I . . . well . . ."

"You couldn't help it."

"No! I happened to see."

"Hmmm," she said again.

Nicholas felt himself flushing. "Do you mind if I sit?"

"Sure. You all right?"

"Yeah, fine. I was just hoping . . ." He hesitated.

"You were hoping what? That this was me? That I could tell you who faked the picture?"

He nodded.

"Nick, I've done a lot of weird things in my life but I've never been a call girl—"

"I didn't mean to imply that."

"—not that I necessarily think there's anything wrong with it. It's just something I never wanted to sell. Y'know?"

He nodded again.

She looked down at him. "Is this still that contest you're in?"

He sat down heavily, sinking deeply into the dead-spring sofa. "Yeah. That contest. The Game. I'm tired." He sighed. "I'm sorry. I really should go. I've been enough of a nuisance."

"Hey, it's no bother," she said. "I enjoy you. You're . . . different."

"I guess that's a compliment."

"Oh, it is," she smiled. "Different from the biker guys and sailor-types who have all kinds of swagger and the IQ of toast. Who just want to run up their conquests and be back on the road or open sea." She touched his hair. "Let me go get some clothes on and then we'll talk, okay?"

"Okay. If you don't mind."

"I don't mind at all. Be right back."

Nicholas stared ahead as she went up the stairs. She was different, too, from the women he was used to. Not stuffy or mannered and percolating with false laughter or proper conversation. He liked her. And a big part of him wanted her—not as someone to wear on his arm but as someone to have fun with.

What the hell are you thinking? he asked himself. He didn't even know her. He got up and walked around the room.

There was a Virgin Mary figurine on a lamp table and he picked it up. The head unscrewed and he looked inside. It was a decanter. He put it back. As he stood there, he sniffed the air. He noticed a faint ribbon of smoke rising from the lamp. He peered inside the lamp shade, squinting, and saw a price tag dangling against the bulb. It was turning brown and smoking. He reached in to remove it and burned his finger on the bulb.

"Shit!" he said as he jerked his hand away, nearly overturning the table. He caught Mary and a small, framed photograph before they fell. After setting everything right, he sucked on his finger and walked around the living room. He peeked into the dining room, saw a swinging door which led to the kitchen, and walked in. The room was modest and cluttered with unwashed dishes, boxes of cereal, and trays of cookies. He went to the sink, held his finger under the faucet, and turned the cold water handle. No water came out. He tried the hot water.

Nothing.

He looked around again. There was no water cooler. He looked at the dirty dishes. A couple of days' worth. Maybe the faucet was one of those things they didn't know how to fix but couldn't afford to call a plumber in on. If the bathroom fixtures worked, they could survive.

Maybe.

Curious, he opened a drawer beside the sink. It was empty. He opened another drawer. Also empty. So were all the cabinets and the refrigerator. He went back to the living room and walked over to the lamp table. He picked up the framed photograph and looked at it. It was a photograph of a little girl in a dress. He examined it closely then took the frame apart.

It was an advertisement from a glossy magazine. The text was folded behind the picture.

Son of a bitch, Nicholas thought. He took a breath and quickly replaced the clipping as Christine came back downstairs. She was wearing a pullover dress and was still putting up her hair.

"Want anything to drink?" she asked.

"No, thanks," he said, as light and charming as he could manage. He held up the frame. "You?"

"Yes. First Communion."

"Ah," he said. He fixed her with his gaze, the pleasantness gone. His mouth turned down as he walked toward her. He was still holding the frame. "Do me a favor, Christy?"

She stopped at the foot of the stairs, her uneasiness showing. "Sure, Nick."

"Take the picture out."

"Why? What's wrong?"

"Take the picture out of the frame and show it to me."

"I don't get what—"

"Don't you?" he said. "*Don't you?*"

He stopped, caught himself. There were two women in the house, one Nicholas. Whatever kind of story they decided to tell, their word would go a long way against his.

He handed her the frame. "This is a fake," he said tensely. She set it down on the stairs.

"This whole setup is a fake," he went on. "Why?"

Christine swallowed, came close, and put her hands on his shoulders. She put her cheek to his and hugged him.

"Hug me," she said.

"Why?"

"They're watching."

He put his arms around her. "What are you talking about?"

"We can't talk here," she said. "They can see."

She pulled back slightly and motioned with her eyes. Nicholas followed her gaze to a smoke detector on the ceiling.

"Mmmm," she said, smiling cheerfully again. "That was nice. So what do you say we go for a drive?"

"I don't think so," he replied.

She took his hand and smiled, though her eyes were concerned. "Oh, c'mon! It'll be fun."

Nicholas yanked his hand away. "No. I'm sick of this whole fucking thing."

"Nick—!" she said.

He walked over to the smoke detector and glared up at it. "You can come out now, assholes, if you're there. Come on out!"

There was a long, disturbing silence. Snorting with indignation, Nicholas turned and looked around the room. There was a tiny fireplace near the sofa. He jogged over and picked up a poker. He ran back and swung the metal bar at the smoke detector, smashing it.

"Now you've done it!" Christine cried. "My God, we're gonna get majorly fucked!"

chapter 26

As she backed against the wall farthest from the front door, Christine pointed ahead. Nicholas hurried over to the door and looked out the window beside it. He saw four thugs jump from the back of a white van—a van with the name *Cable Repair Service* on the side. He didn't know how he'd missed that one, but he had. The men were all holding guns. Nicholas walked over to Christine and stood in front of her. He was still holding tight to the poker.

"*What* have I done?" Nicholas asked. "Blown the rest of the Game? I suppose they're going to kill us now."

"*Get down!*" she shrieked, pulling him to the rug as gunfire shattered the windows and punched holes in the front wall. The lamp, picture frame, and Virgin Mary blew apart, along with other knickknacks scattered around the room.

Squatting very low, Christine pulled Nicholas behind her, toward the kitchen. When they reached the back door, she opened it and they ran out.

Amy was smoking and playing solitaire by flashlight at a weather-beaten picnic table. She looked . . . out of character was the phrase that popped into Nicholas's mind. Like an actor offstage.

"What the fuck?" she said with confused indifference as the two ran out. "Hey, something happening?"

Christine ignored her as she ran along the back of the house. Nicholas followed closely, still holding the poker. It wasn't going to be much use against guns, but it was better than nothing.

"Christ," Nicholas said, "what is this? Who are you?"

"God, wake up!" she said. "This whole thing's a con."

Nicholas wanted to ask her more but they'd reached the corner of the house. Christine stopped. She peeked around the corner. Nicholas did too. He had no intention of trusting anyone's eyes, words, or instincts but his own.

He watched as the first man kicked down the door and blustered into the house, the others covering him. He saw neighbors' faces in dark windows. And he saw his car, intact.

"You got the key?" Christine said.

Nicholas took out his key case. He flipped out the ignition key. "Got it. We running for it?"

"We are," she whispered as the second and third man went in. Then the fourth man entered. "Now!" she said, and the two ran furiously toward the car.

They both ran around to the driver's side, Christine literally diving in and crawling toward the passenger's seat, Nicholas jumping in behind her. He started the engine with a roar, which drew the gunmen out.

"Yo!" shouted the fourth man. "They's here!"

The men started firing, but Nicholas had already floored the pedal and was pulling away.

"Are they going to follow?" Nicholas asked.

"Not 'going to,'" Christine replied. "Are."

Nicholas looked in the rearview mirror as the men swung into the van. He rounded a corner and pressed the pedal to the floor. The car kicked into overdrive, momentarily bucking

Nicholas out of control. He sideswiped a parked car but kept going, running a light. A garbage truck coming crosswise had to slam on the brakes to avoid a collision. It dovetailed, sending up a monstrous squeal and two thick clouds of off-white smoke. The Cable Repair Service van had to spin out to keep from smashing full into the truck, though they clipped the back and lost their front fender as they caromed off. The van didn't stop after the collision. As soon as the driver was able to control the spin, the van roared off in the direction it was facing. The chase was abandoned.

Christine had turned after the BMW's close encounter with the garbage truck and had seen the accident. Nicholas had slowed the car to regain control and had caught most of it in his rearview mirror. He continued ahead at a steadier pace.

"See them?" Nicholas asked.

"Nope. They're gone."

Nicholas crushed the brake to the floor. Christine was thrown forward.

"What the hell are you doing?" she demanded.

"Get out," Nicholas said.

Christine stared at him. "Come again?"

"Get . . . out."

"You've got to be kidding."

"Do I look like I am?"

"Mister," Christine said, "I could've handed you to them. Done what they wanted and been free of them. They find me now, I'm dead."

Nicholas looked at her. "For the last time, get out of my car."

"Oh—tough guy. Okay, well how about this? You kick me out, no one else is going to fill you in on what's going on. Is that what you want?"

He continued to look at her.

"Do you want to know? If I'm gone, you never will. Never."

Nicholas turned and gazed out at the Golden Gate Bridge, which sparkled in the distance. He realized that Christy was right about one thing: she had information he wanted. And he wasn't going to get it if he ditched her for her part in the con. Besides, she did come through for him in the end. He took his foot off the brake and began driving.

"I want to know," Nicholas said. "You talk while I drive us to the police station."

"Uh-uh," she said with surprising vehemence. "No cops. I've got a warrant out—mail fraud. They'll take me in for that, but you won't be able to prove anything else."

"I don't want to prove anything against you," he said. "I want the pricks who are behind this."

"Then no cops. Zero." She took a cigarette from her blouse pocket. While she looked for the dashboard lighter, Nicholas grabbed the cigarette. He tossed it out the window.

"Fine," he said. "No cops. And no cigarettes. Talk."

She sat back and tore her fingers through her hair. "You got any gum?"

"No."

"No. Of course not." She looked out the side mirror and shook her head. "Nothing ever works the way I want it to. I can't believe they didn't take the time to get the house right."

"Who are 'they'?" Nicholas demanded. "You promised answers."

"I don't know who 'they' are," Christine said, mocking him. "Nobody does. I'm an employee."

"Then what the fuck good are you to me?"

"For starters," she said, "I know things. Like who you can trust. Like that your brother was in on this from the beginning."

"That's a lie."

"Oh yeah? I was the waitress on your birthday, remember? Connie told you about C.R.S. that day, remember? Think about it, Nick. Had you ever seen me there before?"

"No," he said contritely.

"That's because I wasn't there before," she said, drumming on her knees. "And fuck it and fuck you," she said suddenly as she pulled another cigarette from her pocket. She pushed in the lighter and opened the window. "Your lungs'll live but I won't if I don't do something to calm myself down." The lighter popped out and she lit the cigarette.

Nicholas didn't stop her. He'd nearly been eaten by dogs, drowned, shot at, electrocuted by his own kitchen light, and flattened by a garbage truck. Christine was right about the smoke.

"It wasn't Connie's fault," she said after a long drag. She exhaled out the window then took another drag. "He thought it was his only way out. They fleeced him pretty good."

"How? Extortion?"

"Nothing that crude," she said, blowing out more smoke. "They did the same thing to him as they did to you."

"What are you talking about?"

Christine looked at Nicholas. Her expression was one of pity. "Don't you know?"

"If I did, would I have asked?"

She took a puff. "Have you checked your bank accounts lately? No, I guess you haven't. You've been too busy with us."

"What do you mean?"

"I mean that that night in your office, I got the number to your private line. That gave C.R.S. remote access to your computer. You already gave them everything else."

"I did? When?"

"When you took their tests. They got your handwriting, voice samples, psych info."

Nicholas made a face. "That's nuts."

"You think so? They used all that stuff to figure out your

passwords. The ones you thought no one could ever figure out. Feingold, the guy who signed you up? That incompetent-looking zhlub? He did five years for hacking Citibank. They only had to keep you distracted while they broke into the financial network and transferred your holdings to dummy accounts."

"No way," Nicholas shook his head. "Impossible." He glanced at the dashboard clock then took out his cellular and punched in a number using his thumb. His palm grew sweaty as he held the phone to his ear.

"Why do you think they're willing to shoot you now?" she asked. "Scratch that: *wanting* to shoot you now?"

"Overseas operator?" Nicholas said. "Would you please dial Allgemeine Bank, Zurich."

"Because they're finished with you," Christine said. "They want you to disappear—permanently."

"Bull," he said. "Absolute, complete bullshit. No—" he said into the phone. "I'm not talking to you, Operator. I'm sorry."

Nicholas drove onto the Bridge. He wasn't sure where he was going but he knew he had to get away. San Francisco was no longer safe for him.

The bank call was put through and Nicholas selected his option from the menu. An operator came on after a short while.

"*Guten tag,*" Nicholas said. "*Englisch Bitte.*"

"Yes, sir," said the operator.

"Blue-two-backslash-five. Mother's maiden name: Miller. Six-nine-zero D-as-in-David. Yes. I'd like the balance please." He listened. His brow drooped and his lower jaw fell. "That's impossible! When did—"

Nicholas listened. They got it that morning. All of it.

He hung up the phone.

If they got the U.S. accounts, then it was true: he was completely flat. Busted.

But there was one thing they hadn't taken from him. One thing they *couldn't* take from him. Unlike his father, Nicholas wasn't a quitter. And as long as he had anything — even if it was anger — that was enough to keep him going.

chapter 27

As soon as they crossed the Bridge, Nicholas stopped at the first convenience station they could find. Neither he nor Christine had eaten, and while she went to get food he called Sam Sutherland at home. He was out for the evening, so he left a message on his office voice mail.

"You've got to call me on my mobile as soon as you get this," Nicholas said, "whatever time it is. I really need your help. I don't know how, but these C.R.S. people have drained all my accounts. Now they're trying to kill me. You tell the cops that I've got one of them with me. We'll make her testify. I know how this must sound, but it's true—all of it. I'll be out of town. Whatever happens, thanks, old friend."

Nicholas hung up as Christine returned with an armload of food.

"The clerk? She, uh—she cut your card in half. American Express wouldn't accept it and when she called they told her it was reported as stolen."

"Jesus," Nicholas said. "These peckers are thorough."

"Yeah, well—that's the truth. So this is my treat." She handed him a coffee and dropped a half dozen boxes of cookies and cereal on the seat. "That was the one thing in the house that was mine," she added. "The cookies and sugar cereal. God, I love stuff that's bad for me."

"I've noticed." Nicholas pulled from the parking lot and continued north.

It didn't take long before the lights of the city and the fear of being shot at were well behind them. After explaining to Christine that they were heading to a cabin which had been in the Van Orton family since the 1930s, Nicholas drove in silence, highway giving way to two-lane roads giving way to dirt roads. They passed a logging truck and headed into the hills. The only stops they made were at convenience stores, Nicholas draining cup after cup of coffee to keep himself awake.

They reached the cabin shortly before dawn, their arrival greeted by lightning flashes as a storm rolled in from the Pacific.

"Nick, this is gorgeous," Christine said as she looked out at the dark, starlit sky and its reflection in the lake.

"That it is." He snickered. "Worse thing comes to worst, I can always move up here and live like Grizzly Adams. The cabin's just about the only thing I own free-and-clear."

He opened the door with a key he kept under a rock. While he lit a fire in the fireplace, Christine made coffee in the small kitchenette.

"How often do you come here?" she asked.

"Once every two or three months. I do some fishing, hiking, swimming. Clear my head."

"I could get into that."

"What? The recreation or my head?"

"The former," she replied. "I'm not sure I'm equipped to go exploring through the latter."

"I guess it's a pretty fucked-up place," he said. "It's amazing how you think you've got everything together because you're making money. Then all of a sudden you find yourself buck naked in a manner of speaking, and you start to realize how un-together you really were."

"I wouldn't beat myself up over that," Christine said. "We all get so damn caught up in what we *have* to do that we never stop and think about what we *should* be doing."

"You won't get an argument from me about that," Nicholas said. "Not anymore."

She handed him his coffee and looked up at him. "What?"

"I didn't say anything."

"Oh," she said. "Two sugars," she said as she dropped the cubes in his mug.

"Thanks," he said. He walked from the kitchenette and stared at a row of family photos on the mantel. He picked up one of his father and himself holding up fish they'd caught. It was one of the few times he could remember the elder Van Orton smiling. He used his index finger to rub dust from his father's face. God, what he'd give to go back to that time as an adult. Just be able to talk to his dad, find out what he was thinking and what made him happy or sad. Just for a night.

"My name's not Christine," she said as she walked up behind him. "It's not my real name."

"It doesn't matter," Nicholas said, replacing the photo. He took a swallow of coffee. "It really doesn't matter."

"Nick—it's just money," she said. "You should be glad you're alive."

"Should I be?" he said. He turned to look at her. "Is that your professional opinion?"

"What's wrong?"

"Nothing. Nothing except that I'm standing here wondering what the hell I'm doing here with you."

"I thought we came to an understanding—"

"Oh, and that makes everything better? Tell me. How many times have you done this? I'm interested."

"Done what?"

"Scams. Con games. How many?"

"I don't know," she said sheepishly. "A lot."

"I'll bet. Well, let me tell you something, Christine or Christy or whoever the hell you really are. Whatever kind of nickel-and-dime shit you're used to, this is more than just me. This is pension plans and payrolls. Your employers took over six hundred million dollars."

Her eyes fell. She looked sick and frightened. Nicholas did not hurt for her.

"You helped ruin peoples' lives, Christine. How do you live with—"

The cellular chirped and Nicholas put his coffee on the mantel. He snatched the phone from the table.

"Yes?"

"Mr. Van Orton, it's Sutherland."

"Yes, Sam. Talk to me."

"Well, when I got your message I was disturbed, to say the least."

"Great. What I need to know is what do we do?"

Christine stepped closer. "Who is it?" she whispered.

"I've been on the phone for an hour already," Sutherland said. "I don't know what's going on, but your funds are intact."

Nicholas straightened. "Come again?"

"Nothing's been touched."

"How can that be?" Nicholas asked. "I checked them myself."

"Then someone was pulling your leg," Sutherland said. "Listen—where are you?"

"Who *is* it?" Christine demanded.

"My attorney," Nicholas said hotly. "He says nothing's missing."

"Who's there with you?" Sutherland asked.

"The person I told you about on the phone," Nicholas said. "The one who was working for C.R.S."

Christine shook her head. "Don't believe him, Nickie. He's in on it."

Nicholas regarded her hotly. "Sam, hold on," Nicholas

said as he touched the mute button. "Sam Sutherland has represented me for my entire professional life. You don't know what the fuck you're talking about!"

"I know that there are a couple of key numbers I couldn't get from you that weren't on any of the forms. Like the combination to a safe in your home. The alarm code. Where do you think those came from?"

"Mr. Van Orton?" Sutherland said. "I have another call. Tell me where you are and then stay there till I come and get you. Are you at the beach house? The desert house? The cabin?"

Nicholas had to fight the urge to punch something. Why should he believe this woman? She'd tried to con him once, why not again? And why would Sutherland turn on him? Greed? Envy?

It's been known to happen, he told himself. People have betrayed friends, family, and nations before. Until he could figure out who he could trust, Nicholas decided to do what he'd promised himself earlier: he'd trust only himself.

He unmuted the phone. "Sam, I'll get back to you," he said, then disconnected the call. He stared at Christine. "We're going to have to get out of here. If he's against me, he'll be sending someone here to check."

She smiled. "You know what? I wouldn't worry about it."

He gave her a questioning look. "What do you mean?"

"I mean it's out of your hands."

Suddenly, the room began to turn. His head started to throb and his breath grew short. He dropped the phone as he spun toward the mantel.

"The . . . coffee!" he gasped as his vision dimmed. "You . . . you . . ."

"Drugged you? You betcha." She leaned over him and lit a cigarette with an ember from the fireplace. She tossed the ember back and blew smoke in his face. "Y'know, Nickie, most people don't realize how easily cellular calls can be intercepted. Those calls you made to B of A, Switzerland?

You were talking to us. You filled in the blanks. Access codes, passwords, stuff even Sutherland didn't have." She dropped ashes on the floor beside his head. "We have them now. Dummy."

His head was still pounding and the room was blurry but Nicholas reached for the woman. He wanted to rip the smile from her face. She laughed and backed away. He tried to stand but fell, clutching his gut and wailing. The pain was intense. His head felt like he'd OD'ed on MSG, his belly felt like it was on fire, and his eyes felt like they had thumbs pressed into the sockets.

"It's over, Nicholas. And in case I never see you again—and I expect I never will—good-bye. It's been fun." With that, she turned and left.

Nicholas felt the cookies and coffee come back up his throat as his vision swirled and his mind slipped deeper into blackness.

And then there was nothing.

chapter 28

Nicholas awoke with his head pounding, his arms and legs feeling as if they were filled with wet sand, and his eyes sightless. Each breath caused a sharp pain that girdled his torso and ran down his back.

The air was humid, and when he was finally conscious enough to try and move, his hands banged up against something hard on either side of him. He raised them with difficulty and discovered that there was something above him as well. He was in a box.

Or a coffin?

Panic gripped him as he pushed against the covering. It wasn't made of pine, thank God, but felt like particleboard. He pushed harder. He heard it snap and felt it give and after a moment it snapped into several large pieces. He threw them aside and sat up.

The air was dry and it smelled like potpourri—a sea of it. White light seeped through cracks in the walls and flies buzzed around him. He was too weak to shoo them away. As his eyes adjusted to the brightness he saw that he'd been dressed in a white suit and laid out in a cheap coffin. He also saw three other coffins resting on marble biers, all of them covered with bundles of dry, rotting flowers.

He stood unsteadily and leaned on his own bier as he waited for the wave of dizziness to pass. When the swirling, dark circles cleared, he noticed a red rose fixed to his chest with masking tape. He tore it away and crushed it.

They were twisted, these fuckers. Totally and irredeemably sick. Looking around, Nicholas saw the door. He staggered over, still feeling weak, and threw himself against it. It was made of plywood and swung outward when he hit it. He stumbled into a ramshackle graveyard, small and overgrown with weeds. Birds flew off and bugs swarmed over and he brushed at them as he squinted and turned a slow circle.

By a grave near a rusting, iron fence he saw an old woman sitting with her rosary. She was bundled beneath a black shawl and was staring wide-eyed at Nicholas.

"Where am I?" he asked.

She did not answer.

"I-I'm not going to hurt you. I just want to know what place this is."

She got up and shuffled away quickly. Nicholas shut his eyes, undid the bow tie they'd put on him, and walked after her. It was hot—humid hot—and perspiration dripped down his forehead into his eyes. He felt for his wallet as he walked but they'd taken that. "They" . . . and Christine. How could he have been so careless as to trust her? He was so sharp in negotiating, so canny on the squash court, so smart at banking and investing—how could he have been so fucking stupid?

He wondered if poor Conrad would laugh or cry when he heard about this. How his vaunted brother had fallen for a con job. Not only fallen for it, but continued to fall for it even after he knew it was happening. That took brains.

He heard the sound of traffic ahead. He passed a row of trees, exited the cemetery through a lopsided gate, and found himself on a busy downtown street. The signs were in Spanish; he shook his head slowly.

I'm in Mexico, he thought. *They shipped me down as a dead body and put me in a mausoleum and I don't have an ID or a passport or money or any way to get home.* It would have been kinder if they'd killed him up at the cabin. But these people obviously liked to rob a person of everything, dignity included. That was the Game. Their Game. To strip a person absolutely bare.

But this wasn't the time for self-pity. Not if he ever hoped to get out of here. Spotting a burly police officer directing traffic on the two-lane street, Nicholas brushed himself off and stepped off the curb. The horn of an oncoming truck blared and he jumped back.

The officer looked over. Nicholas motioned for him to come over. He ignored him. This wasn't going to be easy. Nicholas checked oncoming traffic and then walked briskly to the middle of the street.

"Excuse me, Officer, I'm an American. Do you speak English?"

"*Quita de alli!*" he shouted, then shooed Nicholas away as though he were a fly.

Maybe he should have let the goddamned truck hit him. Then he would have gotten some cooperation. "You don't understand. I need help. They took my wallet. If I can call my office—"

The policeman spoke angrily and grabbed Nicholas's arm with both hands.

Nicholas pulled away reflexively. "No, stop that! You don't understand!"

His brow dipping angrily, the officer unsheathed his baton and struck Nicholas in the side. The wind was knocked from his body, his legs wobbled, and he fell to the left, the side where he was hit. He landed hard on his elbow and looked up with an expression of shock and pain.

He saw the baton being raised again and reminded

himself then that this wasn't the United States. Even if someone videotaped what was happening, no one would give a damn. The baton came down again and Nicholas raised his arms in defense. The stick bashed his right forearm and continued down into the side of his skull. Nicholas's ears rang and he could swear he felt his brain slap against his braincase. Cars had stopped and were honking, and as the police officer towered over him menacingly, Nicholas suddenly kicked up and drove the toe of his white suede shoe into the man's groin.

Nicholas got up, his head screaming with pain. He lurched toward the sidewalk and pushed through the crowd that had gathered. He didn't stop or look back. He got his legs back under him and started to run. His head felt warm and he reached up. He was bleeding. His head was throbbing. But he didn't want to stop. He didn't want to end up in a Mexican prison. God alone knew what they'd do to him there.

He finally looked back after running several blocks. The police officer wasn't following him. Maybe he'd gone for help. Maybe not. Maybe they'd find him. Maybe they wouldn't. It wasn't going to do any good to worry about it. He slowed and leaned against a trash can. Blood was dripping into his eyes and he saw a newspaper in the barrel. He pulled off a sheet, balled it up, and held it against his head. There was a bus stop at the end of the next street and he walked over slowly. It felt good to sit down.

Nicholas watched the traffic pass and saw pedestrians stare at him without asking if he needed help. Tears formed in his eyes. A few days ago he'd been on top of the world—wealthy, feared, envied. Now he had the clothes on his back and nothing else. And the clothes weren't even his. He also had one thing more: a colossal headache. Possibly a mild concussion. He had to get help.

Rising slowly, he walked down the street. His step was heavy, uncertain, his legs still weak from the blow to his side. He was down and quite possibly out and he was dressed for burial. But he wasn't ready to lie down and die. He stopped at the first shop he came to, a bakery, and asked for directions to the American embassy. The people there had no idea what he was talking about. Or if they did, they didn't feel like answering.

Why should they? Would he have talked to a homeless man who approached him back home? No. He hadn't, in fact. Back at the airport on the day he went to Seattle.

He continued along the street. It was difficult to focus and the heat made it difficult to breathe. He spotted another police officer directing traffic. He wondered if it was wise to go up to him. Maybe the ball-kicked policeman had gotten to a call box and warned the troops.

Fuck it if he did, Nicholas decided. *This can't go on.*

Nicholas walked over and smiled weakly. "Excuse me. I'm looking for the American—I mean, the United States embassy. Please, sir—please. Can you help me?"

The police officer pointed down the street. Nicholas looked ahead. In the distance he saw the flag hanging limply in the humid morning air. It was still the most beautiful and majestic sight he had ever seen.

"Thank you," he said gratefully. "*Gracias* very much."

Nicholas's smile grew stronger as he ran down the street. He vowed that if they helped him he would never again complain about paying his taxes.

Which reminded him that he didn't have a dime to his name—

Which strengthened his determination to get out of Mexico and find a way to destroy the people who had done this to him—

Which gave him the second wind he needed to keep from collapsing from pain, hunger, and nausea.

chapter 29

Nicholas sat beneath a hardworking ceiling fan and watched the less-hardworking embassy employee read paperwork. Paperwork which Nicholas had spent over an hour filling out.

Maybe these guys wanted to rob him, too, he thought. He'd certainly given them enough information. He'd written down the names and phone numbers—those he could remember—of business associates, family members, and friends in the United States. He'd even listed Elizabeth. It was a bit frightening to think that his former wife was the only one he felt he could trust for sure.

After filling out the forms, he'd waited for nearly two hours for a free counselor. Now that he had one, he was waiting again. Waiting for the slowest reader on earth to finish reading what he'd written.

At least they'd offered him medical attention for his head. Also coffee and cookies. It occurred to him that he'd been eating a lot of cookies the past twenty-four hours or so. More than he'd eaten in the past twenty-four years. God, how he missed Ilsa's cooking.

The middle-aged man took a sip of water. He spoke as he

read. "You've got lots of names here. But no money, no identification or passport." He looked up. "You are in a fix. What happened?"

"Where to begin?" Nicholas said. But that wasn't really the question he was considering. After a couple of hours he was trying to decide whether to tell the man the truth. All he wanted to do was get out of Mexico. The truth might require a longer investigation, checking the SFPD reports, looking for C.R.S. He looked at the nameplate on the man's desk. "Mr. Patterson, it's complicated."

"It always is."

The man's matter-of-fact attitude made up Nicholas's mind for him. Mr. Patterson would only be able to deal with a matter-of-fact crime.

"What happened was, I'm on vacation, alone. I was robbed, at gunpoint. They hit me and ran. Two men. They took my wallet, money. All of it."

"Robbed?"

"That's right."

"What hotel were you staying at?"

Nicholas faltered. "I, uh—I don't remember. I was hit on the head."

Patterson's small eyes darted up to the bandage and then back. "Did you go to the police?"

"Yes, I did. But I don't speak Spanish."

"There *are* police officers here who speak English."

"Apparently not when you look like something the dog dragged in. Mr. Patterson, please. All I need is to get back. Can the embassy lend me the money or phone my former wife and have her wire it down?"

Mr. Patterson smiled for the first time. "How soon do you want to get back?"

"I don't follow."

"I do the pre-screening here," he said. He pointed to an office across from his desk. The door was open and there was a stack of papers nearly a foot high in the corner. "Ms.

Hirschorn there—she does the nuts-and-bolts work. And right now she's on last Thursday's papers."

"You've got to be kidding! Can I make a phone call, reverse the charges?"

"Sure," he said. "But that won't get you a replacement passport."

"Christ! I've got nowhere to stay, no way to eat—"

"I sympathize," Patterson said. "But there's one thing more. You say you were mugged."

"Yes."

"And the muggers didn't take your watch. The one with the gold band."

Nicholas looked at it. It was so much a part of him he hadn't realized it was on. His eyes fell.

"Muggers here usually take everything—including shoes and socks." He folded his hands on the paperwork. "Mr. Van Orton, I don't know what your problem was but how much is that watch worth? A few hundred at least?"

Nicholas nodded. "Why?"

"Because a man with a watch like that doesn't necessarily need a passport, if you get my meaning. I can give you an address. It isn't far from here. Otherwise, there isn't much I can do for you. And when we get to this," he tapped the paperwork, "I can't promise that things are going to go the way you need them to."

Nicholas looked from Patterson to the watch. He took it off and looked at the back. There was an engraved inscription: *On your 18th birthday, your father's watch. All my love, Mother.*

"I'll take the address," Nicholas said.

Fifteen minutes later he was standing in a pawnshop. He came away with one hundred dollars American for it. A couple of days ago he wouldn't have bothered chasing a hundred bucks down the street. Now it had cost him his most precious possession, something that had been a part of him for thirty years.

The desire for revenge bubbled stronger than ever inside.

He went from the pawnshop to a bus terminal four blocks away. The next bus to the border was in an hour. He purchased a ticket then walked to a nearby taco stand and bought himself a very late lunch. The bus came on time and left full. A mother with a young child took the seat beside him. Within a half hour she was asleep, her head slumping against Nicholas's shoulder, the child—a round-faced boy— staring up at him.

Nicholas smiled at the boy. The boy looked away. Nicholas turned and gazed out the window at the crimson and gold sunset. It felt good to be going home.

Like a death, the enormity of what had happened to him was slowly taking root. He'd been taken. Humiliated. Fucked. But this much was also true: whoever these people were, they couldn't have covered every step. He'd find them. At least one of them—that was all he needed. And when he did, he would find a way to take them. Humiliate them. Fuck them.

Fuck them good.

A s Patterson had predicted, a fifty-dollar bribe got Nicholas across the border.

"Pat your pockets like you're looking for your passport," Patterson had told him before he left the embassy. "When you can't find it, shrug and then lean on the table with your left hand. Have the fifty in your right hand folded inside a piece of paper. If the agent asks for some other form of identification, pass him the paper with the money in it."

That's exactly what Nicholas had done. He imagined that half of the money would go back to Patterson. Probably made for quite a nest egg. But this, at least, was a shakedown with some value-added, not like what C.R.S. had done. He understood and even respected that.

Now he was back in the United States, hitchhiking on a deserted stretch of highway outside of Yuma, Arizona. The occasional truck, van, or car roared past over a period of three hours until one of them finally gave him a lift to its destination: Kate and Harry's 24-Hour Diner. The driver offered him a ride to Los Angeles, but he was going to bunk down in his rig for the night and Nicholas didn't want to wait that long. He wanted to get back to San Francisco as quickly and as quietly as possible.

Entering the diner with its sun-faded counter and torn vinyl seats, Nicholas walked slowly along a row of truck drivers. They were hunched low and sitting elbow-to-elbow. Their conversation reminded him of tires on a cobble road: deep, gravelly, and heard for just a moment. It intimidated him. Intimidated this man who had addressed board meetings in convention centers, who had testified in multi-billion-dollar lawsuits, who had roasted others and been roasted at ten-thousand-dollar-a-plate dinners.

Nicholas cleared his throat loudly. "Pardon me," he said as he neared the end of the counter. "If I could have your attention, gentlemen."

The low conversation stopped. Several of the men looked over—not with expressions of curiosity but with expressions of who-the-hell-is-this-asshole-interrupting-my-dinner? Nicholas didn't blame them. Catching sight of himself in a mirror behind the counter, he saw that he looked like a hobo freak in a white suit. But this was his only shot. Not only did he have to take it, he had to make it work. He cleared his throat again.

"I'm truly sorry for the interruption," he said. He dug a hand into his pants pocket. "A couple of days ago I was worth more than half a billion dollars." He slapped his money on the end of the counter. "Now, here's all the cash I've got left in the world." He counted it out. "Eighteen dollars and seventy-nine cents. If anybody's heading to San Francisco, I'd really appreciate a ride. I want to kill the people who robbed me."

There were a couple of snickers. Several men returned to their meals. One man—a blond-haired kid, really—raised his hand. "I'm headin' up that way an' I'll take you on one condition."

"Thanks," Nicholas said. "What's the condition."

"You make all that money legally?"

"I did."

The man grinned broadly. "Okay. Then you're gonna tell me exactly how you did it."

Several of the man laughed. A few applauded.

Nicholas smiled back. "I did it with the following words: you've got yourself a deal."

The ride north was long and surprisingly relaxing. Nicholas knew he was tired, but the strain of the past few days and the aftermath of the drugging had really wiped him out. The driver, Duke Goldstein, proved to be a very cordial and accommodating host. He was taking a shipment of Baskin-Robbins ice cream up the coast, and after Nicholas told him how he'd started buying high-tech stocks in the middle seventies and branched out in the early nineties, Duke resolved to get into the stock market himself.

"But stick with what you know," Nicholas said. "Don't ever let a stockbroker hard-sell you."

Duke promised to take Nicholas's advice, after which he dug out his blanket and pillow and let his passenger catch up on his sleep. Nicholas slept through the evening rest stop and two meals.

They reached San Francisco late in the afternoon of the following day. Nicholas and Duke parted company in the warehouse district—Nicholas giving him tips on a few entertainment stocks he'd been watching—after which the "Broke Billionaire," as Duke had dubbed him, thumbed his way to the outskirts of Pacific Heights. Nicholas walked the remainder of the way. He was rested, it was dark, and he wanted to arrive unseen.

They still had some surprises for him, the fuckers.

When he reached his home, he found the gate tightly closed with chains. There was a *Public Auction* sign hanging from them. Nicholas tore the oak-tag sign down and then ripped it in half. He put his foot in the chains, hoisted himself to the top of the gate, swung over, and dropped down to the driveway. He winced as he landed. His feet already hurt from breaking in his hideous new shoes; this hadn't done his raw heel-backs any good. He didn't move for a moment as he gave his feet a break and listened for sounds of activity. There weren't any. Rising, he walked warily toward the house.

It was dark. Picking up a rock, he smashed in a pane on the front door. He reached through and let himself in. The alarm didn't go off and he looked at the keypad. Dead. Even the battery had been disconnected. He walked slowly through the dark foyer into the living room. The graffiti was gone. He glanced toward the kitchen: so were his appliances. The refrigerator, the microwave, even the coffeemaker. The bank hadn't wasted any time. He didn't think any of this was legal, but who knew what bullshit C.R.S. or Sutherland or someone else had fed them?

He looked out at the yard. The guest house was dark. There was no electricity, of course, but he couldn't see any candles either. He wondered if Ilsa were still here. They'd have to have chased her out to make her leave.

He called her name. There was no answer. He walked through the eerie quiet into the library. The furniture was wrapped in thick plastic and the paintings were all gone. It was as if Nicholas Van Orton had—

Had died, he thought. Maybe he had. Maybe someone had identified his body in the cabin and some fake goddamned C.R.S. funeral home had taken him away. Buried him in Mexico figuring he'd never be heard from again.

Anger repossessed him and he went upstairs. The bedroom furniture was covered over, the art was gone, and the floorboards creaked beneath his feet. Stripping off his white suit, he climbed into the shower and scrubbed vigorously and quickly under the cold spray. There were no towels and all of his clothes had been removed from the closet and dresser drawers. Pulling the plastic from his bed, he lay down naked and went to sleep.

chapter 31

There was no alarm clock to set— Nicholas couldn't imagine what a bank would do with a repossessed alarm clock—but he woke with the birds. He didn't bother to shave. With what he had to wear, why bother? Back in the kitchen, he opened the pantry door and dug around for a mason jar. He unscrewed the lid and removed one thousand dollars in cash. Then he went to the library. Daylight was pouring in the large windows, warm and inviting. He went to the fiction shelf along the back wall and took down a leather-bound edition of Harper Lee's *To Kill a Mockingbird*. He put it under his arm then headed for the front door. He stopped as he passed the kitchen. There was an envelope on the counter. He went over and picked it up. *To Whom It May Concern* was typed on the front.

He opened the envelope and unfolded a letter. It said, *Like my father before me, I choose eternal sleep*. The red signature arrow was still attached to the bottom. Nicholas took it to the stove, turned on one of the burners, touched the edge of the letter to it, then dropped it burning into the sink.

Nicholas walked to the nearest pay phone, near Lafayette

Park, and called a taxi. He took it to the Sheraton Palace Hotel and walked boldly to the registration desk.

"I'm here to see one of your guests," Nicholas said to the desk clerk.

The young woman smiled. "The house phones are located behind you, sir, in the—"

"Please ring the room for me," Nicholas insisted. "Conrad Van Orton. I don't know the number."

"Conrad Van Orton," she said. "One moment, please."

She walked over to a distinguished, gray-haired man with a flower in his lapel. After a moment of hushed conversation the man walked around the counter. He approached Nicholas. "I'm the hotel manager."

"Pleasure to meet you," Nicholas said. "What's the trouble?"

"You're here for Conrad Van Orton."

"That's right. He's my brother."

"Your brother." The man took Nicholas lightly by the arm. "Will you come with me?" he said as he led him from the counter.

"Say, what's this about?"

"It's a private matter." The manager looked around. He leaned close and spoke softly. "A few days ago there were complaints from other guests about noise. We went up to his room—there was severe damage done to it."

"By Conrad?"

The manager nodded. "We did the best we could to accommodate his behavior, but there was an incident a few days ago—a nervous breakdown, they said. The police took him." He reached into his billfold and removed a slip of paper. "They left this address in case anyone came looking for him."

Nicholas looked at the writing on the paper.

"It's a hospital in Napa," the manager said.

"A hospital? What's wrong?"

"I don't know anything more than I told you. I'm terribly sorry."

Nicholas looked at the paper. Napa was a good sixty miles away. Too many cab rides and he wouldn't have any money left. There was only one thing to do. Thanking the manager, Nicholas hired a taxi to take him across the Bridge to Sausalito.

Elizabeth was just putting her daughter on the school bus when Nicholas arrived. She brushed long, blond hair from her head and watched as he paid the driver and walked over.

"Hi," he said.

"Hi," she replied—smiling at first, then growing concerned. "Car in the shop?" she asked as she hugged him. "Suit at the cleaners?"

"No," he said. "I think everything I own's been repossessed."

Elizabeth stepped back, her concern deepening.

"Can we go for coffee?" Nicholas asked.

"Sure," Elizabeth said. She locked up the house and they drove to a small upscale restaurant. Businesspeople were talking deals and eating big breakfasts. Nicholas ordered bottled water. Elizabeth asked for coffee, light, and an English muffin. *Good Morning America* was on an LED TV at each table.

Nicholas fingered a teaspoon with his left hand. His right hand lay flat on his book.

"What's wrong, Nick?" she finally asked. She put her hands on his. "I mean, look at yourself—"

"I know. Look at me." He laughed uncomfortably. "What's wrong? What happened? I don't even really know. Thing is, I have some stuff to try and take care of. I need your car a little while."

"My car."

He nodded.

"Of course you can have it if you need it." She took her

key chain from her handbag and started working the car key off. "You sure you don't want something to eat?"

"I'm sure." He accepted the car key, clutched it tightly in his fist. "I just want you to know, Elizabeth, you're the only person I trust. The only person I *can* trust. If Sam Sutherland or Maria from my office or anyone else calls, don't tell them that you saw me. Lie to them."

"I can do that," she smiled. "I lied to him about how much I needed in our divorce."

Nicholas managed a little smile. "I know. But you were so audacious I told him to go along with it."

The waitress arrived. Nicholas fell silent and looked up at the pale woman as she set out the coffee and muffin, bottled water and a glass with ice. She noticed Nicholas's eyes and pointedly avoided them. He looked away and picked up his water bottle.

"There we go," the waitress said as she finished. "If there's anything else I can get for you—"

"This is open," Nicholas said. He held the water bottle to her. "Someone opened it."

"Yes, sir," she said. "I opened it."

"I can't have this open. I'd like another, unopened. And I don't want ice. I need a glass without ice."

"All right, sir," the waitress said. She hurried away.

Elizabeth cupped one of Nicholas's hands within her own. "Nick, talk to me. You're scaring me."

"Why? Didn't you divorce me because I was such a picky pain in the ass?"

"Among other things," she admitted. "But you were never so angry about it. The woman made an honest mistake."

"What makes you so sure?"

"That's what they do in restaurants. They open cans and bottles. Sometimes they even pour them for you."

Nicholas looked down at her hands around his.

"I'm sorry," he said. "I don't mean to scare you. God, I

don't *want* to scare you." He put his other hand around hers and caressed it. "It's just the last few days—I've been thinking. I've had a lot of spare time, see. And I've been thinking . . . I want to tell you . . . I'm starting to understand why you left me. Maybe I've been resenting you for it, but I want to apologize for all of it. For shutting you out. For working so many damn hours. For not being there when you needed me. For not supporting *your* career. My work always came first. The next ten million, hundred million, quarter billion." He swallowed. There were tears in his eyes. "Like that helps to fill my life now. Anyway, I hope you can forgive me."

"There's nothing to forgive, hon."

"There is, but all I want now is—what I'd like is, it would mean a lot to me if you and I could be friends. If I could have you back in my life in some small way. If you wouldn't mind. If your husband wouldn't mind."

"Of course we wouldn't mind, Nick," she said.

He smiled at her then looked away, embarrassed. He glanced at the TV. And after looking at it for a moment he cried out.

"Nick, what is it?" Elizabeth yelled.

"You bastard!" he screamed at the TV.

A balding figure was holding up a bottle. "You're tired. You've been on the go for days—"

"Feingold, you prick! How did you find me here?"

"Nick, calm down!" Elizabeth said. She turned to the next table. Everyone was looking at them. "He's been under a lot of stress. We're very sorry. Please excuse us."

"Then . . . pain sets in," the balding man continued. "You feel it: the onset of a migraine. If this sounds all too familiar, relief is here at last." He held up a bottle. "Taggarene. For nearly a decade doctors have been prescribing Taggarene to people who suffered from classic—"

"I'll be—oh, man," Nicholas said. He sat back down. "He's an actor. Feingold is an actor."

Nicholas watched as animated graphics of body parts were soothed by Taggarene's painkilling action. Then "Feingold's" face returned in close-up. He held up the bottle again. "So if you trust your doctor, trust Taggarene."

A jingle came on. Nicholas looked at Elizabeth. He pointed at the television. "It's just regular TV. He's an actor."

"Yes," Elizabeth said slowly. "What did you think?"

"I'll explain some day."

"I hope," Elizabeth said.

Nicholas rose. "Look—I've got to get going. Let me drop you back at the house."

"Thanks, but I'm going to stay and eat. It's okay. I'll walk back. It isn't very far."

"You sure?"

She nodded.

Nicholas leaned over and kissed her on the forehead. He reached into his pocket and pulled out a fistful of crumpled bills.

"No," she said, "this one's on me. After all, I am eating it."

"You're a good person," Nicholas said. "Better than I ever deserved."

"You won't get an argument from me," she said.

He touched her cheek and smiled. "Thanks. For everything."

"No problem." She added, dead serious, "Just come back from wherever you're going in one piece."

He gave her a thumbs-up as he picked up his book and slid from the booth. Before leaving the restaurant, he stopped at the cash register.

"Excuse me," he said to the cashier, "do you have a San Francisco yellow pages?"

"We surely do," the elderly woman replied.

"May I borrow it?"

"Certainly," she said. She bent and dug it out from under the counter. She handed it to Nicholas.

"Thanks a lot," he said and hurried out the door.

The cashier watched him go, started to say something, then just scowled.

chapter 32

Nicholas opened the window of the Volvo station wagon and enjoyed the fresh morning air. He drove erratically. The yellow pages were in his lap and he steered with one hand while he paged through the phone book with the other. When he got to restaurants, he stopped. He waited until he reached a red light before examining the book further.

He turned to the section on Chinese restaurants. Seeing "Feingold" again had reminded him of something he'd forgotten. Something he should never have let slip his mind. At once, he spotted the quarter-page ad and the image of the cartoon dragon.

"New Moon Cafe," he read. "Best in Chinatown." He tore out the page, stuffed it in his pocket, and hefted the yellow pages into the backseat. As he turned to look at the traffic light, an arm reached through the window and put a knife to his throat.

"Get out of the car, fucker."

Nicholas held still but his eyes shifted to the left, to a wasted, skittish teenager.

"Open the door and leave it running," the punk said.

"You're making a mistake," Nicholas said.

The knife was pressed harder against Nicholas's throat. His head went back against the headrest, which pressed hard on the cut he'd gotten in Mexico.

The kid looked back at other drivers then back at Nicholas. "I said get the fuck *out* of the car."

"You don't understand—"

"No, *you* don't, motherfucker! Get out of the fucking car!"

"Okay," Nicholas said and shifted in his seat. As he did, he flipped open the hardcover book beside him. It was hollowed out, with a Walther PP automatic hidden inside. He crossed his chest with it and pointed the barrel toward the young man's chin. "Now, do you understand?"

The frightened kid ran off just as the light changed. No one honked. They were so civilized here, across the Bay.

Nicholas went back over the Bridge and stayed on 101. He got off and headed east into Chinatown. He checked the address on the yellow pages advertisement; the restaurant was on Stockton Street. He slowed as he neared the cross street.

"Bingo," he said as he saw it up ahead. He parked on a side street and walked over.

The restaurant was small and cramped, the walls covered with signed celebrity headshots. Nicholas walked up to a tiny old Chinese woman who was folding cartons behind the counter.

"Hi," he said pleasantly.

She nodded. "Can I help you?"

"You have no idea how much I hope so," Nicholas replied. "I'm trying to find someone who orders from here. He's an actor. He does television commercials. I saw him in a headache commercial this morning."

The woman looked up at him, disgusted. "Do you know how many customers we have here? Hundreds. No. Thousands."

"I'm sure. But this is very important to me. I think he orders from here pretty regularly. He had his food delivered to Montgomery Street. Ten nineteen."

The woman shook her head and continued folding cartons, stacking them one inside the other.

"Is there anyone else I could ask?" Nicholas said. He pointed up at the headshots. "He's an actor, but not a famous one I don't think. He—"

Nicholas stopped, his eyes locked on one photograph. Low on the wall behind her, fresh among the photographs browned by grease and age, was a glossy picture of "Feingold." He was looking pretty serious. Nicholas read the inscription. "To May-ling with love, Keith Fisher."

Just then, the old woman turned to answer the phone. As she did, Nicholas leaned on the counter, snatched the photograph from the wall with his fingertips, and left the restaurant.

He turned the photograph over as he walked and smiled. Printed on the back was a list of his credits. There was also a phone number. He stopped at a pay phone and called it. A woman answered.

"Hello," Nicholas said. "This is Kismet Kasting. Is Mr. Fisher in?"

"No, I'm sorry. This is Mrs. Fisher. Can I help you?"

"Perhaps. Your husband's photo was submitted to us late yesterday and—I know this is short notice but we were hoping he could come in for an audition today. We're casting the movie version of *Destry Rides Again: The Musical* and we see he played Claggett at the Candlewood Playhouse."

"Yes! Yes, he did! Does it have to be today?"

"I'm afraid so. The director's in town, and this is the only day he's looking at actors from the Bay area."

"Oh, it'll break his heart if he misses this."

That's a fucking goddamn shame, Nicholas thought. "Isn't there any way we can get in touch with him?"

"His beeper's here on the table. He forgot it when he took the kids to the zoo."

"The zoo," Nicholas said. "How sweet. San Francisco?"

"Yes," she said.

"How many children do you have?"

"Three," she said.

Nicholas slammed the phone in the cradle. He folded the photo into his jacket pocket, went back to his car, and drove to the Golden Gate National Recreation Area.

It was easy finding a lone dad with three kids. They seemed to be everywhere. But he finally caught sight of the right one near the white tiger cage. "Feingold's" kids were gathered around him, making tiger sounds and clawing at one another. There were two young boys and an older girl. Nicholas felt his rage return as he approached the actor from behind.

"Keith Fisher!" Nicholas said grandly. "I love your work!"

The actor turned, smiling and clearly caught off-guard. The cheerful surprise turned to ash, along with his skin color, as he saw and obviously recognized Nicholas.

"Okay, please," he said. "I got my kids."

Nicholas casually opened his white jacket and showed him the gun tucked in his belt. "Get rid of them."

"Where?"

"I don't give a fuck. Lose them."

The actor took a deep breath and turned. "Hey, everyone—ice cream time!" He pulled out his wallet and handed a ten-dollar bill to his daughter. He pointed to an ice cream cart behind them. "I'll meet you in just a couple of secs at the stand over there."

"Oooo . . . Daddy said sex!" said one of the boys.

"*Rrrrr . . . yea, ice cream! . . . rrrr,*" the younger boy yelled as the girl herded them both off. She smiled at Nicholas as she left.

Nicholas smiled back. The smile evaporated as he backed Fisher toward the fence. "Talk. Fast."

"Look, it was just a job. Nothing personal, ya know? I play my part, improvise a little. That's what I'm good at."

"I'm so happy for you. These bastards ruined me. I want them and I'm tired of dealing with peons. I need to talk to whoever's in charge."

"Nobody knows," Fisher said desperately. "Nobody gets to see the big picture." He looked around Nicholas as his son threw rocks at the cage. "Jason, cut that out! Tammy—"

"I see, Dad," she said, exasperated. She walked away from the line to haul little Jason in.

Fisher started as Nicholas grabbed his shirt. "Enough shit. How do I find them? Their offices are empty."

"I don't know. They own the whole damn building. They just move from floor to floor."

Nicholas released him. "They know you. You've worked for them. You can get me in."

"No, I can't. I'm sorry, but—"

"But what? They'll kill you? They'll kill your family? Mister, the way I'm feeling right now—"

Nicholas didn't finish. He couldn't say it, couldn't even think it. He was mad at Fisher and he was going to stay mad at Fisher but he refused to bring anyone else into this.

"You're going to get me in," Nicholas said, more calmly. "Tell them the cops are after you. Tell them you've got to talk to someone, find out what to do. Tell them I'm threatening to blow the whistle."

"What whistle?" Fisher said. "I don't know any names, you don't know any names. That's just my point. There *is* no whistle."

"Then we're going to find one. You get paid. By who?"

"I don't know. I get cash. The envelope is dropped off at the house. Folded inside the newspaper."

"Who hired you? How do you get the jobs, the floor?"

"Over the phone. I'm telling you, I've never met anyone."

Nicholas scowled. "Then, brother, today is going to be a big fat first. Get the kids."

"Why?"

"Because we're going to drop them off at home. The girl rides with me. And after we drop them off, you and I are taking a little drive over to Montgomery Street." He closed his jacket. "Any questions—Mr. Feingold?"

The actor shook his head, then put on a smile as the kids returned.

chapter 33

_____

They took Fisher's station wagon into town.

Nicholas rode in the backseat, under a blanket, with his gun pointed up at the actor. If he tried to bolt, Nicholas swore he'd shoot him. Nicholas wasn't sure he would have, but he would have been tempted. By his careful manner, Fisher demonstrated his own uncertainty about Nicholas's resolve. So far, the actor had been the zenith of cooperation.

The sounds outside the car grew muted. They'd reached the underground garage of the building. They stopped to take a ticket from the guard.

"What are you gonna do anyway?" Fisher asked. "You won't get your money back."

"Maybe I will and maybe I won't," Nicholas said. "What I want right now is to pull back the curtain. I want to meet the Wizard."

"What if he or she doesn't want to meet you?"

"Then it's going to get messy," Nicholas promised.

The car rounded a corner and came down a ramp.

"The guard's watching us like Tiffany Towers."

"Just drive. Park where he can't see."

Fisher did as he was told. He pulled into a spot between

two cars near a pair of elevators. He got out. Nicholas climbed out after he did. He remained crouching between the cars, his gun in hand. He gestured for Fisher to push the button.

Fisher obeyed. When the door opened, Nicholas started to move—then stopped. A large security guard got off holding a walkie-talkie and his gun. These guys were like the Gestapo.

"You're not allowed to be here," the guard said to Fisher.

"I'm, uh—I'm supposed to go upstairs for a fitting."

"I wasn't told about any fittings."

Nicholas moved forward and put the gun to the guard's neck. "You're being told now, buster. Give me the gun, two fingers on the butt."

The guard did as he was ordered. Nicholas grabbed the automatic and slid it along the floor, under the row of cars. Then he took the walkie-talkie and tucked it in his belt, after which he frisked the guard. Finding his handcuffs, Nicholas ordered Fisher to cuff him to the rail.

Trembling, Fisher took the guard and obeyed.

"There's a security camera in here," the guard said.

"I'm not shy," Nicholas replied. "What're they going to do when they see us? Gun us all down?"

"I wouldn't put it past them," the guard said.

"In that case, I'll stand behind you." Nicholas grabbed the guard's hair. "What floor?"

The guard said nothing.

Nicholas put the gun under his chin.

"Twenty-five," the guard said. "But this elevator ain't gonna get you there, college boy."

Nicholas sneered and reached for the key chain clipped to the guard's pocket. He tore it free and sorted through the keys. He found a gold C.R.S. key, inserted it into the slot on the elevator control pad, and hit twenty-five. The door closed. The elevator began to glide upward.

"You'll never get away with this," the guard warned. "These people will fuck you up."

"No worse than they already have."

"You'd be surprised. You got family?"

"They've already fucked with my family."

"All of it?" the guard asked.

Nicholas felt his bowels tighten. *Elizabeth.* "They want to escalate this, I'll escalate," he said, not sure whether or not he was bluffing. "I've got nothing left to lose."

The guard snickered. "I've heard that before."

"Not from me you haven't."

The elevator stopped and the door opened. While Fisher cowered in a corner, Nicholas peered out. The hall was dark and empty. He grabbed the actor by the arm and pushed him out ahead.

"Jesus!" Fisher whimpered as they emerged into the deathly silent corridor.

They stood still for several moments. There were doors up and down the hallway. When no one emerged, Nicholas reached back and pushed all of the buttons in the elevator. Then he pressed down.

"You're fucked!" the guard shouted as the door closed. "You're both fucking fucked!"

Nicholas shook Fisher by the arm. "Where?"

"I told you, they hired me over the phone. I never met anyone."

Nicholas looked up and down the hall. He frowned. "Stop panting, asshole," he said.

Fisher shut his mouth with an audible clap.

Nicholas listened. He thought he heard very faint sounds of conversation coming from the left. "This way," he said, pushing Fisher ahead of him.

They walked for about one hundred yards and the voices were louder. Nicholas listened, following them to a set of swinging double doors. Still keeping a strong grip on Fisher, he pushed him through and went in after. What Nicholas saw caused his eyes and mouth to open very wide.

There was a cafeteria counter along one wall and everyone was here having dinner. The man who'd had the heart attack outside the building. The paramedics who had come for him. Christine's roommate was sitting next to the homeless man from the airport—the cabdriver. The private eye who followed Nicholas was here too. He was just lifting his tray from the counter. Upon seeing Nicholas, he set his tray back down and ran into the kitchen.

Nicholas's eyes continued to look over the faces. The hotel manager from the Nikko. The counter woman from the New Moon Cafe. The desk clerk from the Sheraton Palace. The two businessmen from the squash club. The other businessmen who'd led him to the C.R.S. floor. And Christine. Dear, sweet, devoted Christine.

As more and more of the people began to notice Nicholas, conversation stopped. Nicholas's eyes came to rest on one of the diners. He released Fisher and raised his gun.

Rising with her dirty tray, Christine looked up and saw Nicholas. She stopped chatting with the security guard who couldn't get through the alley. She stared at Nicholas. "Oh, fuck."

Nicholas walked toward her slowly. People quieted. Everyone gave Nicholas room.

"What are you doing here?" Christine asked.

"I didn't like being dead," he said. "Care to try it?"

"Nicholas, okay—you're not going to shoot anyone."

"You sure about that?"

Christine didn't answer.

Nicholas came around the table and pressed the gun to her forehead. "*Well?* Are you still sure I'm not going to blow your fucking goddamn brains out?!"

"Don't move!" someone shouted from behind.

Nicholas swung behind Christine. He hooked his arm around her throat and pushed the gun to her temple. He looked at the two burly security men standing in the door of the cafeteria, just behind Fisher. Both of them held Uzi submachine guns. Held them like they knew how to use them.

"The two men from the elevator," said one of the guards, "come forward."

Trembling wildly, Fisher suddenly shouted and ran for the doors. Both guards reacted with a burst of fire. It wasn't the way it was in the movies: he didn't fly backward, blood spraying everywhere. His churning legs simply stopped and turned to elastic when he was hit. His arms went limp. He stood for a second and then dropped, dead.

The guards did not show any remorse. They kept their weapons trained on Nicholas.

"Brave shooting," Nicholas said. "Two Uzis against an unarmed man."

"Release the girl and put down your weapon," said one of the men.

"That sounds pretty official. I'll take it under advisement." Nicholas leaned close to Christine's ear. "Get us out of here."

"Nicholas, they'll follow—"

"Get us *out*!"

She jerked her head to the right. "Through the kitchen. There's a stairwell."

"Don't move!" the guard warned more forcefully.

"Fuck you," Nicholas said. "Those guns can't cut through the lady and get to me. Certainly not before I poke a few holes in your fat guts."

He started inching her over, still using her as a shield. "Don't try any shit, Christine. I'm definitely not in the mood."

They sidled through the cafeteria to the swinging door of the kitchen. Nicholas elbowed it open and stepped in, still hugging Christine close. The two cooks, both women, were crouched behind the stainless steel counter.

"I'm not going to hurt you," Nicholas told them. "Just stay where you are."

As they crossed the tiled floor to the stairwell, Nicholas picked up a cleaver. He told Christine to open the door and then pushed her in ahead of him. Still keeping an eye on her he wedged the cleaver under the door so it couldn't be opened.

"Now move!" he shouted.

"Where?" she asked, rubbing her throat.

"Upstairs. *Fast.*"

Christine started up the stairs. Nicholas followed. The wind whipped down from the roof just a few yards ahead.

"What do you think you're doing?" she asked.

"I want to know who did this to me. How? *Why?*"

"Why do you think? It wasn't personal, Nick. It could have been any schmuck with a couple hundred million in the bank."

There was pounding on the door. There were gunshots. Nicholas quietly blessed whoever wrote the building code for fireproof, earthquake-proof doors.

"Who's behind this?" he asked.

"I don't know."

He pulled the walkie-talkie from his belt and handed it to her. "Well, we're going to find out. Call them."

"They won't cooperate."

"They will if you tell them I'm going to kill you."

She laughed mirthlessly. "They won't come. They'll let me die first. You're in no position to threaten them."

"You think not? A well-known financial guy holding a woman hostage on a rooftop? You don't think the media will come? You don't think there'll be an investigation? You don't think these bastards will be—"

"Wait a minute!" Christine said. She stopped and turned, the wind stirring her hair. "Where did you get that gun? That's not an automatic."

Nicholas looked at her, startled at first and then guarded. Another trick? "No. It isn't."

"The guard downstairs had an automatic."

"So. What the fuck are you talking about?"

"I'm talking about your gun! Where'd you *get* it?"

"It's mine. I've had it for years."

"But we searched the house."

"Guess you missed it." He glared up at her. The clouds moved slowly behind her. "Enough of your bullshit. Call your bosses and keep walking."

"Wait," she said. She backed away a step. She held up one hand and put the walkie-talkie to her mouth. "Just wait. Okay? Please?"

Nicholas waited.

"Okay," she said again. She really seemed shaken. "Everyone?" she said into the mouthpiece. "Listen. He's got a *real* gun. Do you copy down there? It's a real situation."

"Lady, what the hell are you talking about?"

"Nicholas, you've got to hear me out. This is fake. This is all part of the Game."

"Right. Fuck you too."

"God Jesus *listen* to me. Listen very carefully. I'm telling you the truth now: this is still the Game."

"Horseshit. They just killed Feingold . . . Fisher . . . whatever his fucking name is. They shot him."

"No. They didn't. Think about it. What did you see?"

"I saw them cut him down!"

"You didn't. What you saw were squibs, special effects. Just like in the movies."

The pounding on the door was growing louder. It felt like they were pounding inside Nicholas's head.

"I don't believe you," he said. "Keep moving."

"But I swear it's true! Go down and open that door. Mr. Fisher's right on the other side of that door. He's an actor—"

"Stop talking. Just shut up."

She came back down a step. "Nicholas—"

"Shut *up!*"

"Let me show you!"

"No! You take another step and I'll shoot. You're trying to kill me—"

"You're wrong. If you shoot me it'll be the biggest mistake of your life. Put the gun down."

Now it was Nicholas who took a step back. He wanted to fire. She'd lied to him, drugged him, helped get him shipped to Mexico and left for dead—

"Listen, there was always a safety net. When the taxi went into the Bay—there was a diver waiting in case you couldn't get out. At my house they shot at us with blanks—"

"That's not true."

"It is. It's what you hired us for. Nobody touched your money. Nobody stole anything. They're waiting on the other side of that door with champagne. All your friends. It's a celebration—"

"No!"

"Open the door and you'll see. Your brother's here. Conrad—he's there. It's your birthday party. One long celebration."

"*Stop it!*"

"Please, Nicholas," she said as she continued backing him down the steps, toward the door and the pounding. "Let me show you."

"Don't move—"

She kept moving. "I have to show you." She bent and wriggled the cleaver free. She stood facing him. He backed away. She came closer.

"No!" Nicholas raised the gun toward her head. She moved toward him with the cleaver. His hand trembled, finger tightening on the trigger. "I said don't! Get away!"

Suddenly, the door swung inward. Nicholas turned reflexively and fired. The shot echoed through the stairwell momentarily deafening him. He didn't hear the magnum of champagne explode but he saw it. He watched it throw foam and glass in all directions. Watched as his brother stumbled backward, blood on his tuxedo, blood splattered on the face of Fisher who was standing to Conrad's right.

Watched as his brother fell to the floor motionless.

The deafness from the shot faded in time for Nicholas to hear Christine scream.

chapter 34

"He's dead," Fisher said as he rose from beside the body of Conrad Van Orton.

Nicholas was numb now. His only sensation was a thought: that he would give anything to stop time and take it back. Take back the shot, take back the panic and disbelief that caused it, take back everything. It didn't matter that they had done this to him, that Conrad and C.R.S. and the Game had driven him to the brink. He had just shot his own brother.

"You killed him," Fisher said, staring at Nicholas with disbelief.

Christine took the gun from his hand. "Why did you do it?" she asked him quietly. "I told you—why didn't you listen?"

"We're all going to jail," Fisher said. "All of us for the rest of our lives. Accomplices to murder." He looked at Christine. "How could you let this get so far out of hand?"

"He wouldn't listen to me," she said. "I tried telling him."

Nicholas heard their words but they seemed to come from a distance. What did it all matter now? Conrad was dead. He listened to the loud pounding of his heart, to his rapid breathing, to the sounds of his own life. His *life*. The very thing that his fear had stolen from Conrad. He stared blankly at the open door, saw only his brother's shocked look as he fired. If only he could take it back.

"What have I done?" he said weakly, sobbing now.

He killed his brother. His kid brother. The kid who had looked up to him, who wanted to be like him. Well, now he wanted to be like Conrad. He wanted to stop the pain.

He wanted to die.

Turning, Nicholas ran up the stairs to the roof.

"Hey!" someone shouted. "What's he doing?"

"Where's he going — ?"

"Stop — !"

Nicholas ignored the shouts. He reached the roof. There were rows of sawhorses, stacks of wood, and other construction materials on either side. He raced through them, through the chill night toward the edge of the building. San Francisco was spread out before him, beautiful and inviting. Like Heaven.

I'm so sorry, Connie! he sobbed.

He didn't stop. He saw his father standing on the roof of the house, hesitating. Father hesitated about too many things. He hesitated about giving love and finding new ways to challenge himself after he had made one million dollars and then another and another. He had even hesitated about killing himself. Nicholas wasn't like that. He refused to procrastinate. He ran toward the low wall at the edge and he kept on running until suddenly there was no roof beneath him. His left foot hit the air and dropped and then the rest of him followed. He kicked as he fell, his arms pinwheeling at his sides. He screamed and wished, suddenly, that he could take the jump back. Nicholas's terrified cry became one with the air rushing loudly past his ears. The ground and the lights came up quickly. In the darkness below he suddenly saw what looked like glass. It sped toward him and he crashed through it and it didn't slow him at all. But then something suddenly appeared beneath him, growing by the instant—

He hit the airbag with a bounce that sent him back up nearly six feet. He landed on his shoulders, the air knocked out of him, his head spinning. Under the glow of the streetlights he felt fabric all around him, smelled the rubber beneath it. The cushion began to deflate quickly, easing him to the ground. His back ached, his head was swimming, and he was completely confused. As the bag sank away from his ears he heard voices.

"Let's go! Make sure he's all right—see if he's okay."

Nicholas turned his eyes to the right as people wallowed toward him through the folds of the cushion.

One of them bent beside him. He was wearing a black jumpsuit with the letters C.R.S. in gold on his chest.

"Take it easy," the woman said. "Can you hear me?"

"Yeah," he said. "What—what's going on?"

The woman turned around and made an okay sign with her fingers. She smiled and looked across Nicholas. There was another worker, a man, on the other side.

"Let's get him up," the woman said.

They helped Nicholas to his feet as, around him, the enormous bag settled to the ground. They walked him onto the tile floor of the atrium as the door of one of the elevators opened and Conrad ran out.

After making sure that Nicholas could stand, the C.R.S. employees withdrew. Nicholas blinked, uncomprehending, as Conrad walked toward him.

"What . . . is this . . . ?" Nicholas asked.

Conrad smiled. "This is your birthday gift, Nickie."

"My . . . my birthday—"

Conrad put his arms around his brother. His chest was still stained with red. Nicholas felt his anger returning. It burned through the whirling disorder of the last several minutes.

"My—birthday?" Nicholas rasped. He pushed his brother away. "All of this . . . still the Game?"

Conrad nodded.

Nicholas laughed and cried at the same time. He was relieved, he was furious, he was shocked, he was tired. He ached everywhere from the fall. He wanted to kill his—

No. He didn't want to kill his brother. Nicholas looked at Conrad and wept openly and put his arms back around him.

"I don't believe this," Nicholas wheezed. "Jesus—you're out of your goddamn mind."

Conrad put his mouth beside Nicholas's ear. "Maybe. But I had to do something. You were becoming such an asshole."

Nicholas closed his eyes and held Conrad even tighter.

A moment later, Nicholas heard the *ping* of another elevator. He opened his eyes as Elizabeth and Ilsa walked out wearing tentative smiles. They were followed by Sutherland, Maria, and the C.R.S. staff and players. They all gathered around the Van Orton brothers, hugging them and offering congratulations to Nicholas for having made it all the way to the end—though one of the C.R.S. employees confessed that they were still putting the finishing touches on the breakaway glass in the atrium while Nicholas was upstairs in the cafeteria.

"We were sweating bullets," he said. "Real ones—not the fake ones our guys were shooting."

Nicholas looked at Conrad. "Speaking of which, how'd you manage the fake death? No one knew about my gun."

Conrad grinned. "The C.R.S. techies were all over your house with metal detectors. They found your li'l ole handgun and loaded it with blanks."

Nicholas stood there shaking his head. "Unbelievable. I hate the hell out of all of you for doing this to me, but you did an incredible job."

"Wait!" Conrad said. "The best is yet to come!"

chapter 35

The ballroom of the Sheraton Palace was crammed with well-wishers and the participants in what was being called the Rebirth-day of Nicholas Van Orton.

There had been clean clothes waiting for him in a suite upstairs. After a shower and a long think—mostly about how he, like Ebeneezer Scrooge, was lucky to be given a second chance at life—Nicholas had gone downstairs to join the party. Even Anson Baer was there. He hadn't known about the Game but had been invited to the birthday celebration by Sutherland. Like a good sport, he'd come.

Nicholas told him they'd have some business to discuss the following morning. About his remaining to run the company he'd co-founded. Baer said he'd be happy to stop by the office to talk with an old friend.

"A perplexing friend," Baer admitted, "but one of many years and, I hope, of many years to come."

"You can count on it," Nicholas told him.

After Baer wandered away, Nicholas saw Ilsa approach Conrad. If he wasn't mistaken, it was the first time he'd ever seen their old nanny in a ball gown.

"You look ravishing," Nicholas said.

"Thank you," she replied. "And thank you," she said to Conrad. "This was a brilliant idea. I hope we'll be seeing more of you."

"Without a doubt," he said.

Conrad squinted uncomfortably as Ilsa reached out to straighten his hair.

"Your brother isn't the only one who has needed fixing," she said.

"I'll get a haircut," he promised.

She regarded Nicholas. "Good night. I will see you at home."

"Good night," Nicholas said. "And thanks." He watched her go. "Where was she when I came back from the dead?"

"Here. Ordering room service and watching pay-per-view. She was a real sport. Not only did she handle the travel arrangements down to Mexico City but she insisted on accompanying you. As your nurse. You were very sick, you see. She also stayed down there to make sure you got out of the country."

Nicholas made a face as one of the Dallas businessmen walked over.

"Congratulations," said Jerry Gill, shaking Nicholas's hand. "That was the best one I've seen—ever."

"Ditto," said Ted Thurston. "You did amazing, Mr. Van Orton."

Someone tapped Nicholas on the shoulder. He turned to face "Feingold."

"Hi there," Fisher said. "All I want to say is, thank God you jumped. If you hadn't I was supposed to follow you and throw you off in a blind fury."

"I'm just glad I jumped off the right side," Nicholas said. "That's why you had all the construction stuff—"

"No one's ever died on us yet."

"Well, thank you," Nicholas said, offering his hand.

"You're welcome," Fisher said. "But like I told Connie here after I mourned his passing, I was just doing my job."

"You went above and beyond the call of thespian duty," Conrad remarked.

"Thank your wife and kids too," Nicholas said to Fisher. "They, uh—they *were* your wife and kids, weren't they?"

"You bet. And members of SAG, Equity, and Aftra all. Sometimes my wife does the work in these things and I'm the house-husband."

Nicholas shook his head as Fisher moved away and the other players came over to congratulate him—and to thank him for being so aggressive.

"You made us think on our feet," Christine's roommate said. "That's when this job is really fun."

"For whom?" Nicholas asked.

After they left, Nicholas looked around. "Hey, Connie—where's that kid who attacked me? He was pretty damn good. I really believed him."

Conrad seemed puzzled. "Who?"

"The car-jacker. The kid who tried to steal my car."

"What car-jacker?"

Nicholas stared at him. "He was real?"

"C.R.S. didn't send him."

The two men laughed nervously as Sutherland ambled over.

"Bravo, young man," the attorney said. "You'll both have to tell me what this was all about sometime."

"You mean you weren't in on it?"

"Not until the night you called from the cabin. Connie rang me then to tell me not to worry about you or your fortune, that they were both safe. Until that point I was fully prepared to have you committed to the finest mental health facility available. I mean that sincerely—don't thank me."

"You warm my heart," Nicholas said—a moment before his heart truly did warm. He smiled as Elizabeth came over with her husband and daughter.

"You okay?" Elizabeth asked.

"Yeah. Fine. Really."

"I was worried for a while there."

"Me too."

"We have to head out," Elizabeth said. "I just wanted to say good-bye."

"You're going? Well, thanks again." He smiled at the pretty young girl beside her. "Good to see you, Rachel—and you too, Mel," he said, shaking the hand of Elizabeth's husband.

"Glad everything worked out," Mel said sincerely. "And I know Elizabeth is too."

"Thanks. Oh, and Elizabeth—I'll get your car back to you. Right now it's over at Fisher's house."

"I'm not worried," she said, kissing his cheek. "Not anymore."

Nicholas winked at her appreciatively as she turned and left.

"Happy birthday, Nicholas," she said over her shoulder. "And many, many happy returns."

"I'll call," Nicholas said. "I really will. Bye, guys."

Conrad put his arms on his hips. "Y'know, I've always liked her."

"Yeah, Connie. I know."

"You should never have let her get away."

"Yeah, Connie. I know."

Conrad's eyes suddenly shifted. "Uh-oh," he said.

"What?" Nicholas felt a stab of concern. The Game *was* over, wasn't it?

"There's one thing I wish I could get rid of."

Nicholas followed Conrad's eyes. A waiter was walking toward them with a tray. On it was a nearly two-inch-high stack of computer paper. When the waiter arrived, Conrad lifted it off.

"What's that?" Nicholas asked.

"The itemized bill. Hefty mother. Cars, blanks, actors, breakaway glass, spray paint, composite photos, plane fare to Mexico, dog food—it's all there."

Nicholas looked at his brother. "How about we split it?"

Conrad grinned. "You serious?"

Nicholas nodded.

"Fair enough," Conrad said. "Hey, I'll even give us a discount."

"What do you mean?"

"Consumer Recreation Services seems like a good investment," Conrad said, winking. "I decided to buy into it."

Nicholas shook his head. "Well, since you're actually making money off of me, you can spring for the price of sending a messenger over to the office. And speaking of dog food, what was the deal with those dogs? They nearly chewed my ass off."

"Oh, that was pretty clever. They're trained to respond to Christine. Wouldn't bite anybody's ass without her express permission. Whenever C.R.S. uses them, she's got to be part of the action."

"Jeez, Christine," Nicholas said. He turned quickly and looked around the ballroom. "Where is she?"

"I saw her a minute ago. She was headed out the door. I think she has a plane to catch."

"Does she?" Nicholas said. He excused himself and ran toward the exit.

His tired legs carried him faster than he thought they would. He was in the street in a minute, looking north and then south. He spotted the woman just as she was getting into a cab.

"Christine!" he yelled.

She looked back, hesitating.

Nicholas jogged over. "You're leaving," he said.

She nodded. "I . . . I generally don't mingle with clients after the Game is over."

"Is that all I am? Just a client?"

She looked down. "That *was* quite a fall you took. I'm glad to see you're okay."

"Yeah, I'm okay," Nicholas said. "Except that I almost

didn't get a chance to say good-bye. You were good. I mean—bad, but good."

"Thanks."

"I never did get your real name, though, did I?"

"No, you didn't. It's Claire."

"Pleased to meet you, Claire." He held out his hand. She shook it. Her hand felt warm . . . nice.

"I hear you've got a plane to catch."

"Mm-hmm. There's another gig starting next week in Australia. Just a walk-on, but work's work."

"I see. Well, how about dinner sometime? Would that be breaking any kind of rules?"

"Not the company's," she said. "But you don't know anything about me."

"Then why not tell me about yourself?" Nicholas asked, ignoring the annoyed look he got from the taxi driver.

"Like what's my favorite color?"

"No. Like where are you from?"

"Originally, Colorado."

"Big family or small?"

"One brother, one sister, both younger."

"The overachieving elder sibling," Nicholas said. "Single?"

She nodded.

"Boyfriend?"

She shook her head.

"Underwear?"

"Always, except when I'm working."

"Ever late for work?"

"Never. That's why I've got to go . . . now."

"Will you let me keep you company to the airport?" Nicholas asked.

"You'll miss your party."

"I'll miss—*their* party," he said, nodding back toward the hotel. "I've got the engagement I want. My treat," he added.

The young woman smiled. "You've got yourself a deal, Mr. Van Orton."

"Call me Nicholas," he said as he followed her into the cab and they headed toward the airport.

And a life that had once seemed so urgent, so driven, suddenly felt so slow that a vacation in Australia seemed not only desirable but necessary. . . .